BEGINNING WITH THE BIBLE

A CLASS ABOVE

a child's further lessons
in knowing God

The New Testament

TnT Ministries

CHRISTIAN FOCUS PUBLICATIONS

TnT Ministries (which stands for Teaching and Training Ministries) was launched in February 1993 by Christians from a broad variety of denominational backgrounds who are concerned that teaching the Bible to children be taken seriously. They were in charge of the Sunday School of 50 teachers at St Helen's Bishopsgate, an evangelical church in the City of London, for 13 years, during which time a range of Biblical teaching materials has been developed. TnT Ministries also runs training days for Sunday School teachers.

© TnT Ministries
29 Buxton Gardens, Acton, London, W3 9LE
Tel: +44 (0) 20 8992 0450 Fax: +44 (0) 20 8896 1847

Published in 1999, reprinted 2004, by Christian Focus Publications Ltd. Geanies House, Fearn, Tain, Ross-shire, IV20 1TW
Tel: +44 (0) 1862 871 011 Fax: +44 (0) 1862 871 699

Cover design by Douglas McConnach

This book and others in the TnT range can be purchased from your local Christian bookstore. Alternatively you can write to TnT Ministries direct or place your order with the publisher.

ISBN 1-85792-445-2

All Scripture references are from the Good News Bible except where indicated.

Beginning with the Bible

New Testament Bible Lessons for Young Children

Beginning with the Bible is a series of lessons designed to teach small children the main Bible stories. It is a sequel to **First Class,** which introduces young children to basic concepts about God and his world. **Beginning with the Bible** consists of two books, one covering stories from the Old Testament and one from the New. This book contains 5 lessons about the Christmas story, 15 about the life and teaching of Jesus taken mainly from Luke's gospel, and 7 stories about the early church taken from the Acts of the Apostles. There are a further 2 lessons from Luke that can be used if Easter is late.

Beginning with the Bible can be used anywhere where there are 2½ - 4 year old children - at home, in a play group or church crèche. The lessons can be taught by parents or anyone else who has the care of young children, without any special teacher training being required.

Why teach young children Bible stories?

Children of this age have already demonstrated their remarkable capacity to learn. They love stories and are quick to identify with what they hear. They are able to enjoy loving relationships with parents and other significant adults. They also have the ability to develop a simple trust in God.

We believe that the Bible is God's word to mankind, and that it contains everything we need to know in order to be reconciled with God and live in a way that is pleasing to him. Therefore, we believe it is vital to teach small children what God has to say, so that they can learn who he is and what he has done. We need to lay a foundation of knowledge about God that will enable them to develop a relationship with him and grow into Christian maturity in later years.

How do young children learn?

Children in the 2½ - 4 year old age range cover a broad range of abilities. Many of them will attend a play group or nursery class, so will be used to other children. They love to practise skills and learn mainly by repetition.

Most children of this age will have a good basic vocabulary, but care needs to be taken to use appropriate language. Words should be simple and sentences short and the teacher needs to avoid Christian jargon, e.g. small children do not understand the word *sin*, but easily identify with *all the naughty things I do*. This age group is full of questions and learns through exploration and involvement.

Visually, young children love bright colours and simple images. Therefore, pictures used in teaching sessions must be big, clearly drawn and uncluttered. At the younger end of the age range hand/eye co-ordination is at an early stage, so colouring in tends to come out as a scribble, whereas many 4 year olds are able to produce a creditable effort. Do remember that girls develop skills earlier than boys. Even though the end result may look disastrous the children still enjoy it and can take pride in what they have created. They cannot use scissors, but are able to glue with help.

Children enjoy making things to keep or take home that remind them of what has been learned, even if they have had very little part in their making. Therefore, much of the craft work outlined in the lessons needs to be prepared in advance of the time when you are teaching the children in class.

Children of this age have a short attention span (5-7 minutes maximum) and the lessons are designed with this in mind. Therefore, it is important to choose a suitable time for the teaching. The children need time to settle down after parents have left, but still be fresh enough to listen and learn. In order to gain maximum benefit from the session there needs to be 1 adult for every 3-4 children. Opportunities for reinforcing the lesson should be found during play time.

How to use this book

The lessons have been designed so that they can be used at home or as a short slot in a longer session. They can be taught as an interlude in a church crèche or play group, or at home on a Sunday afternoon or other convenient time of the week.

Each lesson is set out in the same way. The title is followed by the **Lesson aim**, which details what the child is expected to learn from that particular session. This is followed by a section entitled **Preparation**, which sets out the Bible passage for the story, with some questions to help you think about what the story is teaching. This bit is easy to skip, but for the sake of the children and yourself please be committed to making adequate spiritual preparation, as well as preparing the visual aids and craft work. To prepare a lesson properly takes 2-3 hours.

The next section consists of a detailed **Lesson plan**, which must be thoroughly understood and learned, so that the children can be taught without reference to the lesson material. The Bible story is written out in suitable language as a guide only; it should **not** be read to the children. This section includes ideas for visual aids and 2 or 3 activities to help reinforce the lesson.

Give time to teaching the children, letting them contribute and ask questions, but keep it as short as possible, otherwise their attention will wander and the opportunity be lost. Try to strike a balance between the lesson being fun, and yet serious. Your attitude is very important - they will take their lead from you.

Remember always to check activities and crafts for potential **safety** problems. Although every care has been taken in the preparation of this material to avoid safety hazards, you need to be aware of possible problems in the class area for the children. This age group can be very boisterous!

Each lesson ends with a **Prayer**. Although we sometimes find the idea of prayer difficult to understand, for children it is often very natural. Closing eyes and holding hands

together is not necessary, but it helps them to concentrate. Young children find a prayer drill helpful, done to a count of 3, e.g.

1. shake your hands out in front,

2. bring your hands together in front

3. bring your hands up to your chest and close your eyes.

Try to get them to understand that God is listening and wants to hear our prayers. Many children of this age will be happy to pray out loud and this should be encouraged. Never force any child to pray.

At the back of the book you will find details of how to make some of the suggested **Visual aids.**

What results?

We believe that, carefully and prayerfully used, these lessons will lay a foundation of Bible knowledge that will result in the child learning who God is and what he has done. As with *First Class*, we hope that **Beginning with the Bible** will result in:

1. The child developing a simple trust in God.

2. The parents learning to be relaxed, natural and confident in teaching their child from the Bible.

3. The child entering Sunday School/Junior Church ready to learn and take part in a more traditional lesson.

4. The teacher growing in his/her own relationship with God. You cannot teach even a 3 year old something you do not fully understand!

Teaching small children is an important job and is worth doing well, even though it is time-consuming if done properly. Jesus said: *'Let the little children come to me, and do not hinder them, for the kingdom of God belongs to such as these.'* (Luke 18:16). If Jesus thought children important, who are we to deny them access to his word which brings life?

Contents

Contributors: Trevor & Thalia Blundell, Rachel Garforth-Bles, Annie Gemmill, Kathy Manchester

Artist: Andrew Blundell

The Birth of John the Baptist

Lesson aim: to see that John's birth marked him out as God's special messenger.

Preparation

1. Read Luke 1:5-25,57-66.

2. Answer the following questions:
   - what do we know about Zechariah and Elizabeth? (v.5-7)
   - what instructions are given about John's upbringing? (v.13-16, cf. Numbers 16:1-4, Judges 13:2-5)
   - what job would John do? (v.17, cf. Malachi 4:5-6)
   - did Zechariah believe the angel? (v.18-20)

3. Pray for the children you teach, asking God to help you teach them his word clearly.

4. Choose appropriate visual aids.

Zechariah was a Jewish priest. He worked in God's temple. His wife was called Elizabeth. Elizabeth and Zechariah were very old. They had no children. This made them very sad.

One day Zechariah went to work at the temple. It was his turn to burn incense on the altar. So he went into the temple. While he was there God sent an angel to give him a message. When Zechariah saw the angel he was very frightened. The angel said to him, *'Don't be afraid. God has heard your prayers. Elizabeth will have a little boy . You must call him John. When John grows up, he will be a special messenger for God.'*

Zechariah said to the angel, *'How can I be sure this will happen?'* The angel said, *'You will not be able to speak until the promise comes true.'*

Zechariah had stayed a long time in the temple. The people wondered what had happened. When Zechariah came out, he could not speak.

Later on, Elizabeth had a baby boy. Her family and friends were so happy about this. When the baby was a week old he was given a name. Zechariah couldn't speak, so he wrote down the name. Zechariah wrote: *'His name is John.'*

Then Zechariah was able to speak again and everyone praised God.

Prayer
Dear God, thank you for giving Zechariah and Elizabeth a little baby. Thank you that he would grow up to tell people about you. Amen.

Visual aids
Pictures from a Child's Story Bible.

Activities
1. Photocopy page 8 for each child to colour.

2. Make a cone figure of Zechariah. Photocopy page 9 on card for each child. Prior to the lesson cut out the pieces and place in an envelope for each child.
   The children colour the head, feet and the belt around the middle of the body. The hat and robe are left white. Help the children fold the body into a cone shape and glue it together. Place the head on the body by placing the long tab through the hole at the top of the cone. Staple or glue the base of the tab to the inside of the body front. Glue the hat onto the head and the tabs of the 2 feet to the inside of the body front so that the feet stick out.

God gave Zechariah and Elizabeth a baby boy.

When he grew up he was known as John the Baptist.

Cone People - Zechariah and Paul (see page 67)

Requirements
For Zechariah cut out the body, Zechariah's head, turban and feet.
For Paul cut out the body, Paul's head and head-dress.

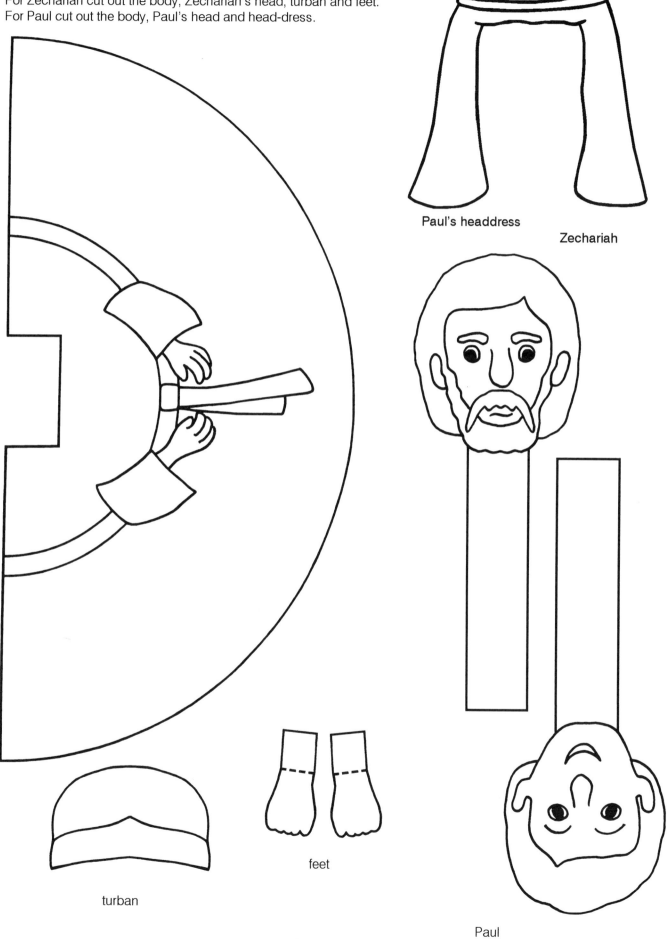

Paul's headdress

Zechariah

turban

feet

Paul

The Annunciation

> **Lesson aim: to see that Jesus' birth marks him out as the Son of God.**

Preparation

1. Read Luke 1:26-56.

2. Answer the following questions:
   - what do we learn about Jesus? (v.31-33)
   - what was Mary's response to Gabriel's message? (v.28-38)

3. Think about Mary's willingness to obey God, regardless of consequences. As an unmarried woman she would carry a social stigma and might be rejected by both family and society.

4. Pray for each child you teach, that God will open their eyes to who Jesus is.

5. Choose and prepare visual aids.

Remind the children about last week's story - the birth of John the Baptist. Elizabeth had a relative called Mary. Mary was a young woman, not old like Elizabeth. Mary lived in Nazareth. She loved God and she was going to marry Joseph, who loved God too.

One day, when Mary was by herself, an angel called to see her. Do your remember last week how the angel came to tell Zechariah that he and Elizabeth were going to have a baby? This angel came to tell Mary something like that too. But Mary was to have a baby in a very special way, because he would be the most special baby of all. He would be Jesus, God's own Son.

Mary was so happy, she went to see Elizabeth. Elizabeth was very happy to see her, and the baby inside her was happy too. Mary was so happy that she sang a special song to God.

Finish by reminding the children why Jesus was the most special baby of all.

Prayer

Dear God, thank you for sending Jesus to be our saviour. Amen.

Visual aids

Pictures from a Child's Story Bible or paper bag puppets of Mary, Gabriel and Elizabeth.

1. Draw clothes on the paper bags with felt tips.

2. Cut out hands from light card and sellotape to the corners.

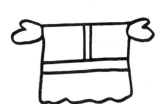

3. Cut out heads with necks from light card, colour and sellotape to the top of the bags. If wished, hair can be made from strands of wool glued to the head.

Activities

1. Photocopy page 11 for each child. Provide torn up pieces of gummed yellow paper for the angel and torn up pieces of another colour gummed paper for Mary. The children stick the coloured paper onto the 2 figures to make a collage.

2. Play musical statues. The children pretend to be Mary and perform various actions to the music, e.g. sweep the floor, dust, wash the floor. Each time the music stops they have to be afraid, just like Mary when the angel came. Finish by asking the children to dance to the music to show how happy Mary was when she visited Elizabeth.

God sent the angel Gabriel with a message for Mary.

The angel said, 'You will give birth to a son, and you will name him Jesus.' Luke 1:31

The Birth of Jesus

Lesson aim: to learn that God became man.

Preparation

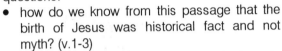

1. Read Luke 2:1-7.

2. Answer the following questions:
   - how do we know from this passage that the birth of Jesus was historical fact and not myth? (v.1-3)
   - why was it necessary for Jesus to be born in Bethlehem? (Micah 5:2)
   - do you know how babies were wrapped? (v.7) The baby was placed diagonally on a square of cloth and 2 corners were turned over his body, 1 over his feet and 1 under his head. The whole was fastened by strips of cloth wound round the outside.

3. Think about the wonder of God becoming man.

4. Ask God to help you teach this story clearly and simply.

5. Choose and prepare visual aids.

Remind the children of the previous story - the angel telling Mary she was to have a baby boy. Mary and Joseph got married. It was nearly time for Mary to have her special baby. The king decided he wanted a list of everyone in the country. Each family had to go to their own town. Mary and Joseph had to travel a long way from Nazareth to Bethlehem, which was Joseph's town.

It was a very long and tiring journey. When they finally arrived it was late at night. Joseph went from door to door asking for somewhere for them to stay. Because there were so many people in Bethlehem to be counted, there was nowhere at all to stay. They finally came to a door where the man said he didn't have any room in his inn, but there was some clean straw in the stable where the animals slept and they could stay there.

Very gently Joseph took Mary to the stable. Later that night the very special baby was born. His name was Jesus. Do you remember why he was so special? Mary wrapped Jesus up warmly and laid him on some clean straw in the manger (explain what a manger is).

Prayer

Dear Lord Jesus, thank you for coming to earth as a special baby to be our saviour. Amen.

Visual aids

Pictures from a Child's Story Bible or models.

If using models build up a crib scene over the next 3 stories, adding various characters each week. Make sure the characters are not breakable, as the children like to play with them. Use a cardboard box for the stable and duplo figures or yoghurt pot people (see page 83). The stable needs straw (or shredded wheat) on the floor and a manger made from cardboard.

It is helpful to have a baby doll to show the children how the baby was wrapped and a cardboard box with straw to put the baby in.

Activities

1. Act out the story.

2. Photocopy page 13 for each child. Prior to the lesson cut off the strip containing the baby and cut out the baby. The children colour the picture and the baby. The children glue the baby into Mary's arms or the manger.

3. Sing the first verse of *Away in a Manger*.

Mary gave birth to her first son, wrapped him in strips of cloth and laid him in a manger.

The Word became a human being and, full of grace and truth, lived among us.   John 1:14

Lesson 4

The Shepherds

> **Lesson aim: to teach that the good news of Jesus is for everyone.**

Preparation

1. Read Luke 2:8-20.

2. Answer the following questions:
   - what was the good news?
   - who was the good news for?
   - how did the shepherds know the good news was true?
   - who receives peace on earth? (v.14)

3. Think about the peace Jesus brings (Romans 5:1).

4. Pray for the children you teach, that they may realise that Christmas is about Jesus.

5. Choose and prepare visual aids.

Use the visual aids from the previous lesson to remind the children of the birth of Jesus.

The same night that Jesus was born, there were some shepherds looking after their sheep in the fields nearby. Suddenly the dark sky grew bright and an angel appeared. The shepherds were very frightened. The angel said to them, *'Don't be afraid. I've come to tell you good news. A baby called Jesus, your Saviour, was born tonight in Bethlehem. You'll find him wrapped up warmly and lying in a manger.'*

Many other angels began to sing, *'Glory to God in heaven and peace on earth.'*

So the shepherds hurried to Bethlehem. They found Mary and Joseph in the stable and the baby lying in a manger, just as the angel had said. They were very happy to see the special baby and they knelt down and worshipped him. Then the shepherds went back to their sheep. They told everyone they met about the wonderful things they had seen and heard.

Prayer

Dear Lord Jesus, thank you for coming to be my saviour. Amen.

Visual aids

Pictures from a Child's Story Bible or models.

For models see the instructions for lesson 3 (page 12). Add shepherds and an angel. Make sheep from pipe cleaners and cotton wool. As well as the stable you need a separate table to be the field.

Activities

1. Act out the story.

2. Photocopy page 15 for each child to colour. Glue cotton wool balls on the sheep bodies and colour the light strip with a bright yellow crayon. Stick some gummed silver stars in the sky.

3. Make an angel mobile. Photocopy page 16 on card for each child. Prior to the lesson cut out the shapes. Using a needle and cotton attach the angels to the rectangle so that the angels hang at different levels. The angels and rectangle are marked with X at the appropriate points. Fold the rectangle in half along the dotted line, glue together and make 2 holes at the dots. Thread a length of wool through the holes and tie to make a hanging loop.
   The children colour the angels or decorate them with gummed stars and pieces of doilies.

his very day in David's town your Saviour was born - Christ the Lord!

Luke 2:11

Angel Mobile

When Jesus was born the angels sang praises to God.

X   X   X   X

Lesson 5

The Wise Men

Lesson aim: to learn that Jesus is the Son of God and should be worshipped.

Preparation

1. Read Matthew 2:1-12.
2. Answer the following questions:
   - how many men were there? (v.1)
   - why did they go to Jerusalem, where the king lived? (v.2-3)
   - why did Herod want to know where Jesus was? (v.8,13)
   - where was Jesus living when the wise men found him? (v.11)
   - do you know the significance of the 3 gifts? Gold signified kingship, frankincense divinity, and myrrh for a man who would die (myrrh was used in the embalming of bodies). The 3 gifts are the reason why the wise men are portrayed as 3 in number, although there is no definite evidence for this.
3. Think about Jesus being worshipped by Jew (shepherds) and Gentile (wise men). He came as Saviour of the world and he is the only way to God.
4. Ask God to help you teach the children that Jesus is truly God.
5. Choose and prepare visual aids.

Lesson

Using the crib scene remind the children of the previous 2 weeks' stories - the birth of Jesus and the shepherds coming to worship him.

When Jesus was born a bright star appeared in the sky. Some wise men saw this star. They realised that a special king had been born. They followed the star all the way from their own countries.

The wise men came to the king's palace in Jerusalem and asked to see the special baby. The king did not know where the baby was, but the priests who studied the Bible (God's word), knew where the baby was to be born. Many years before, one of God's messengers had told God's people that Jesus would be born at Bethlehem. This was written down in the Bible.

So the wise men went to Bethlehem and found Mary and Joseph with the baby Jesus. The wise men gave Jesus presents and worshipped him, because Jesus is the Son of God.

Prayer
Dear Lord Jesus, thank you that you are God. Amen.

Visual aids
Pictures from a Child's Story Bible or models.

For models see the instructions for lesson 3 (page 12). Make figures of the 3 wise men and add them to the crib scene as the story progresses. The wise men need paper crowns and presents. Make a star from gold paper or use one that goes on top of a Christmas tree.

Activities
1. Allow the children to play with the figures in the crib scene. Get them to repeat the story.
2. Photocopy page 18 for each child. Prior to the lesson cut out the 3 wise men and the star and place in an envelope for each child. Give each child a sheet of A4 coloured paper with, *'They saw the child with Mary his mother, and they fell down and worshipped him. Matthew 2:11'* written along the long side. The children glue the figures of the wise men and the star onto the coloured paper. Colour the wise men and star.
3. Make a crown. Cut out the 2 halves of the crown from an A4 sheet of card (see diagram). Cut off the 2 black triangles and discard.

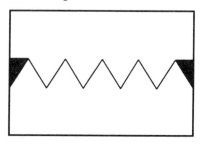

Write on one half, 'Jesus is my king.' Staple the 2 halves together at one end. The children colour and decorate their crowns with coloured stars, pieces of silver foil, coloured paper shapes, etc.

Fit the crown onto the child's head and staple/sellotape the 2 ends together.

Lesson 6

Jesus is Baptised

Lesson aim: to see that Jesus was shown to be the Son of God at the start of his earthly ministry.

Preparation

1. Read Matthew 3:13-17, Mark 1:1-11.

2. Answer the following questions:
   - what was John's message? (Mark 1:4)
   - does repentance involve more than saying sorry? (Mark 1:4-5)
   - which OT prophet was John like? (Mark 1:6, Luke 1:17, 2 Kings 1:8)
   - how did John react to Jesus' request for baptism? (Matthew 3:13-15)
   - what signs were given and to whom? (Mark 1:10-11, John 1:32-34)

3. Think about the meaning of true repentance. Do we ever confess our sins to God without intending to stop sinning?

4. Ask God to open the children's eyes to who Jesus is.

5. Prepare visual aids.

Let us make a river scene (see visual aids).

Refer back to the pre-Christmas lesson about the birth of John the Baptist.

When John grew up he became a preacher. He taught the people that they were **all** sinners and needed God's forgiveness. (Discuss with the children what sin is - the naughty things we do.)

The people came to John to be baptised to show that they were sorry for what they had done. They wanted to stop doing the wrong things and do good things instead. (Discuss baptism and how John performed it.)

John told the people that another preacher would come who was far greater than John. This preacher would give them the Holy Spirit.

One day Jesus came to John and asked John to baptise him. John recognised that Jesus was the mighty preacher he had told the people about. John did as Jesus asked.

Straight after Jesus was baptised God's Spirit came down from heaven in the form of a dove and rested on Jesus. God spoke to Jesus from heaven saying, 'You are my own dear son. I am pleased with you.'

Stress the lesson aim at this point.

Prayer

Dear Lord Jesus, thank you for coming to make us your friends. Please help us to be really sorry when we do naughty things. Amen.

Visual aids

You need a large piece of card or cartridge paper (A3 or larger), colouring pens and gummed paper for the sun and trees. Photocopy page 20 on card for the figures of John and a man. Draw the river, bank and hills on the cartridge paper (see diagram). Cut a slit 4.5 cm long in the river for the man. Reinforce the slit with sellotape. With the children, stick/glue on the trees and the sun (see templates on page

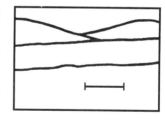

20). Using a split pin paper fastener attach the figure of John to the left of the slit. Join the 2 pieces of John's arm through the dots at the elbow with a split pin paper fastener. Using split pin paper fasteners join the arm to John through the dots at the shoulder and to the man through the dots at hand and head. Stick the figure of the man through the slit. At the appropriate point in the story pull the tab at the bottom of the figure of the man to duck him in the river.

Activities

1. Photocopy page 21 for each child. Prior to the lesson cut off the strip with the dove and cut out the circle. Cut out the marked section on the picture. The children colour the dove and glue cotton wool balls onto the clouds. Using a split pin paper fastener attach the dove circle behind

the picture at X so that the dove flies out of the cloud.

2. Make a dove finger puppet. Photocopy page 20 on card for each child. Prior to the lesson cut out the head, body and finger strip and place in an envelope for each child. The children colour the head and body. Roll the head into a cone and glue the flap inside (this can be done round a finger).

Roll the finger strip around a finger, cut to the required length and glue. Attach the rolled finger strip to the underneath of the body using sellotape.

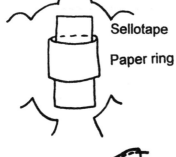

Sellotape

Paper ring

Glue the neck inside the head at the top so that the back of the head completely covers the neck.

finger strip

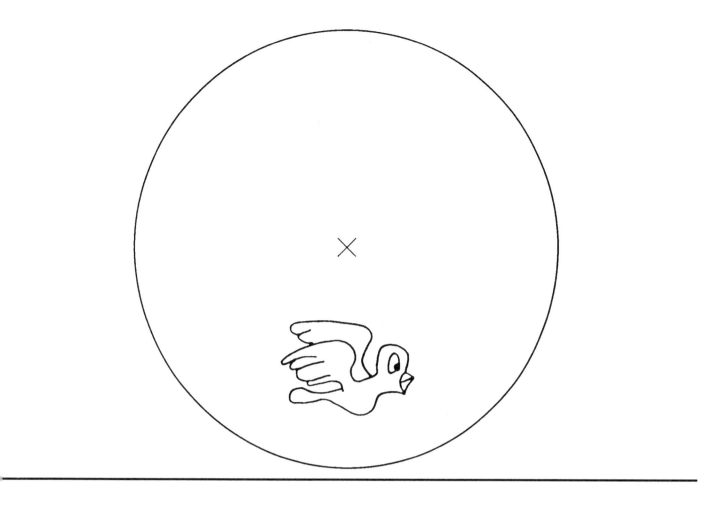

Jesus was baptised by John.

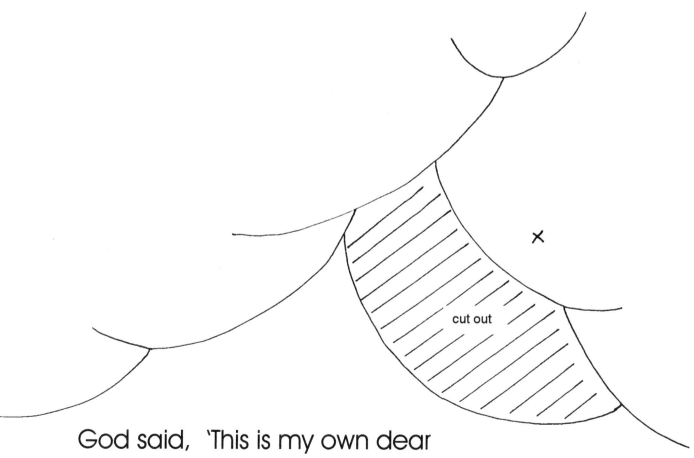

God said, 'This is my own dear
Son, with whom I am pleased.'

Matthew 3:17

Jesus Chooses His Disciples

Lesson aim: to learn that Jesus calls people to follow him.

Preparation

1. Read Luke 5:1-11.

2. Answer the following questions:
   - why did Jesus get into the boat? (v.1-2)
   - what do verses 4-5 tell us about Peter's relationship with Jesus?
   - what happened when Peter did what Jesus said? (v.6-7)
   - what was Peter's reaction? (v.8-9)
   - what did the 4 men leave to follow Jesus? (v.11)

3. Think about the importance of obeying Jesus. Are you prepared to give up whatever is necessary to follow him?

4. Pray for the children you teach, that they will understand the importance of obeying Jesus.

5. Choose appropriate visual aids.

Start by asking the children if they can remember who the story was about last time. Today's story takes place soon after Jesus was baptised.

One day Jesus was at the lakeside, teaching the people about God, and they were crowding around him.

There were two fishing boats by the lake and the fishermen were washing their nets. Jesus got into one of the boats and asked the fisherman to row out a little way. The man's name was Simon Peter, and he did as Jesus asked. Simon's brother, Andrew, was also in the boat. Jesus taught the people from the boat.

When Jesus had finished speaking, he told Simon Peter to row farther out and let down his net to catch fish. Simon Peter explained that they had been fishing all night and had caught nothing, but he did

as Jesus told him. There were so many fish in the net that it was in danger of breaking.

Simon Peter called his friends in the other boat, James and John, and they rowed out to help. There were so many fish that both boats were full. The men were astonished. Simon Peter fell on his knees before Jesus. Jesus told Simon Peter not to be afraid. Then he asked the 4 men to go with him to help him.

After they had rowed ashore the men left their boats and followed Jesus.

Prayer

Dear Lord Jesus, thank you that you want us to be your friends. Amen.

Visual aids

Pictures from a Child's Story Bible.

Activities

1. Catching fish. Make 2 fish out of coloured tissue paper for each child.

Make fishing rods of sticks with a length of string tied to one end. At the end of the length of string attach a piece of sellotape rolled in a circle with the sticky surface on the outside. This will allow the tissue paper fish to be picked up.

2. Make a sea scene. Each child requires an A4 sheet of blue paper with, *'Jesus asked 4 fishermen to go with him and help him.'* written along the top and, *'They left everything and followed Jesus. Luke 5:1-11'* written along the bottom. Provide cut-outs of fish, weed, shells, etc. from magazines for the children to glue onto the paper. Fish cut out of coloured plastic or cellophane are very effective.

Lesson 8

Jesus Heals a Paralysed Man

Lesson aim: to learn that Jesus can forgive sins because he is God.

Preparation

1. Read Luke 5:17-26.

2. Answer the following questions:
   - who was listening to Jesus teach? (v.17,19)
   - who had the faith? (v.20)
   - were the Pharisees and teachers of the Law correct? (v.21)
   - how did Jesus demonstrate his ability to forgive sins? (v.22-25)
   - what does this miracle teach about who Jesus is?

3. Think about the wonder of being forgiven. Do I forgive other people when they sin against me?

4. Pray for the children you teach, that they will go to Jesus for forgiveness.

5. Prepare visual aids.

One day Jesus was teaching people in a house like this *(see visual aids)*. The house had so many people in it that there was no room for anyone else.

There was a man who was paralysed. *(Explain what it means to be paralysed.)* He had some friends who had heard that Jesus could make sick people well. They brought their friend to Jesus, but they could not get into the house. So they went up onto the roof and made a hole in it. Then they lowered their sick friend down to where Jesus was. Jesus saw that the man's friends believed that he could heal him. He looked at the man and said, *'Your sins are forgiven.'*

The people listening were amazed. They thought, *'How can Jesus forgive sins? Only God can do that.'* Jesus knew what the people were thinking. To show that Jesus could forgive sins he told the sick man to get up and walk. The man got up immediately and went home with his friends, praising God for what had happened.

Stress the lesson aim at this point.

Prayer

Dear Lord Jesus, thank you that you forgive us when we are truly sorry for the naughty things we do. Amen.

Visual aids

House with paralysed man and 4 friends (see page 24).

Activities

1. Photocopy page 25 for each child. Cut the page in half and cut out the window. Cut around the door so that it will fold back along the dotted line. Glue the 2 pieces together at the top, bottom and sides so that the door can be opened to show the man on his stretcher. The children colour the pictures. Give each child a scrap of material to stick over the man as a blanket.

2. Ask the children to lie down on the floor. Tell them that they are like the paralysed man. You are going to give them various instructions and they are only to respond when you say, *'Forgiven.'* The required response is to jump up and dance around. Use different instructions, e.g. *'Get well'*, *'Walk'*, *'Stand up'*, etc., interspersed with *'Forgiven'*. Play it as a game.

Visual aids

House Take a large cardboard box and cut out a door and a window. Cut flaps in the top that can be pushed open to lower the paralysed man on his stretcher.

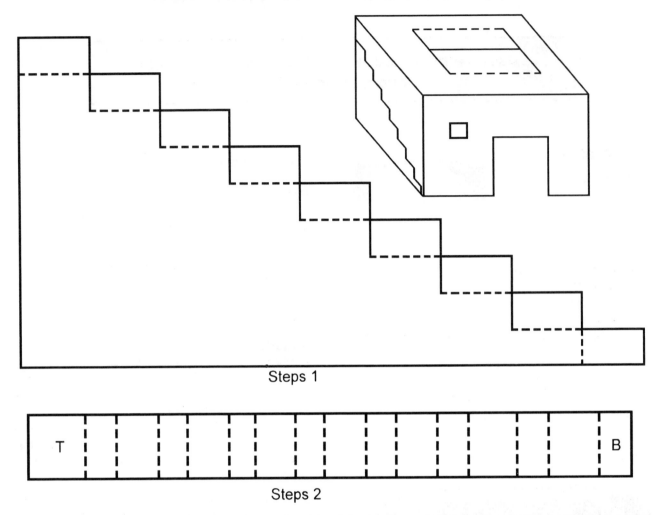

Steps 1

Steps 2

Stairs Take a piece of card the same size as the side of the house and draw in the steps, starting at the back and an inch below the top and ending at the bottom and an inch from the front. Then draw in a second zigzag line an inch above the first (see diagram). Cut out along the upper line, cutting down to the lower line along the solid lines as on the diagram. The dotted lines on the diagrams are fold lines. Cut out a strip of card one inch wide and concertina fold to fit the zigzag line of the steps. Attach the strip of card to the top of the folded over prongs of steps 1 with staples. Attach the finished steps to the side of the house using large split pin paper fasteners.

People You need yoghurt pots or plastic drinking cups, egg cartons, scraps of material, wool, rubber bands, cotton wool, sellotape, glue, pens. Cut the head from an egg carton and sellotape onto a yoghurt pot or plastic cup. Draw on a face. Dress with a piece of material secured round the middle with wool or a rubber band. Tuck the bottom edge of the material inside the bottom of the pot. Attach the head-dress in similar fashion to the robe. Glue on cotton wool as a beard if required.

Make a stretcher from the lid of a margarine tub. Attach string to the 4 corners so that the paralysed man can be placed on the stretcher and lowered into the house through the roof flaps. Place a piece of material on the stretcher so that the man can roll it up and take it home.

Jesus Heals a Paralysed Man

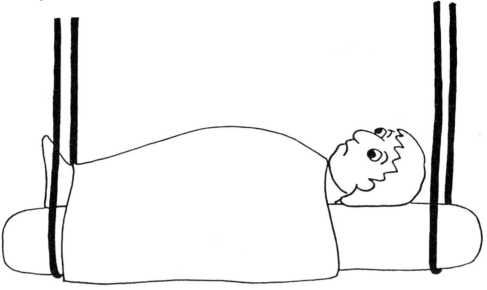

cut

Jesus said, 'Get up, pick up your bed, and go home!'   Luke 5:24

Lesson 9

The Parable of the Two Houses

Lesson aim: to teach the importance of doing what Jesus says.

Preparation

1. Read Luke 6:46-49.

2. Answer the following questions:
   - why did Jesus tell this parable? (v.46)
   - who was he talking to? (v.17-20)
   - did both the wise and the foolish hear Jesus' words?

3. Think about the importance of putting Jesus' words into practice. Is there any area of your life where you are failing to do this?

4. Pray for the children you teach that God will give them a desire to hear about Jesus.

5. Choose appropriate visual aids.

Remind the children of the previous story about Jesus healing the paralysed man. What did we learn about who Jesus is? If Jesus is God should we listen to what he has to say?

One day Jesus was with his friends, the disciples, surrounded by a large crowd of people. The people had come to see Jesus because they had heard about him making people well. They wanted to hear what Jesus had to say and to ask him to make them well too. So Jesus taught the people what it means to follow him and be his friend. He told them the following story.

There were 2 men who each decided to build a house.

One man dug deep and built his house on solid rock. The other man did not bother with all that hard work, but built his house on sand. They both had fine looking houses.

After a time there was a great storm. The rain came down in torrents and the whole area was flooded. And what happened to the two houses? The house that was built on rock stood firm, but the house that was built on sand collapsed when the sand was washed away.

Jesus said that the people who listen to him and do what he tells them are like the man who built his house on the rock. When the hard times come these people will stand firm. They will remain Jesus' friends. But those people who do not do what Jesus tells them are like the man who built on sand. When the hard times come they will turn away from following Jesus.

Talk about where we find Jesus' words - in the Bible - and why it is important to listen to the Bible stories.

Prayer

Dear Lord Jesus, thank you for the Bible, which teaches us about you. Please help us to do what it says. Amen.

Visual aids

Pictures from a Child's Story Bible.

Activities

1. Make a story box.
   Photocopy page 27 on card and page 28 on paper for each child. Make up the boxes following the instructions on page 27. Cut out the 4 pictures from page 28 and place in an envelope for each child.
   The children colour the pictures and glue them round the box in the order of the story.
   Use the story box to revise the story.

2. Photocopy page 29 on card for each child. Cut along the thick black line round the top and sides of the house. Fold along the dotted line to make a stand-up card. Cut out 4 windows and 1 door from coloured gummed paper and place in an envelope for each child (see templates on page 28).
   The children colour the picture and glue the windows and doors onto the house.

side 4

1. Cut out, score and fold along dotted lines.

2. Glue side 4 to the remaining 3 sides.

3. Glue the top flaps inside the sides to make a box open at the bottom.

The Parable of the Two Houses
Luke 6:46-49

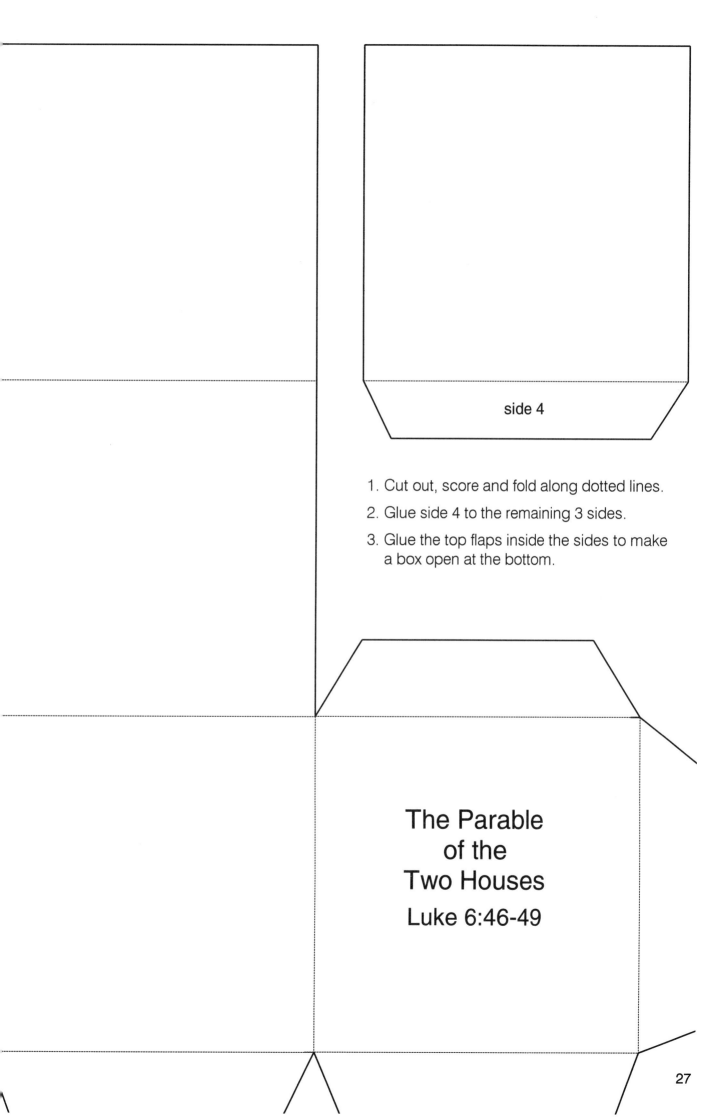

Two men each decided to build a house. The wise man dug deep and built his house on solid rock.

The foolish man did not bother with all that hard work. He built his house on sand.

When the rains came the house on the rock stood firm, but the house on the sand fell flat.

Jesus said that wise people are those who listen to his word and do what he says.

Templates for door and windows (see page 29)

Cut one door and 4 windows from coloured gummed paper for each child.

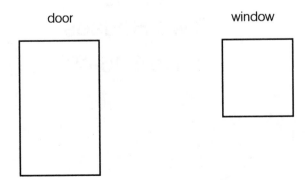

door

window

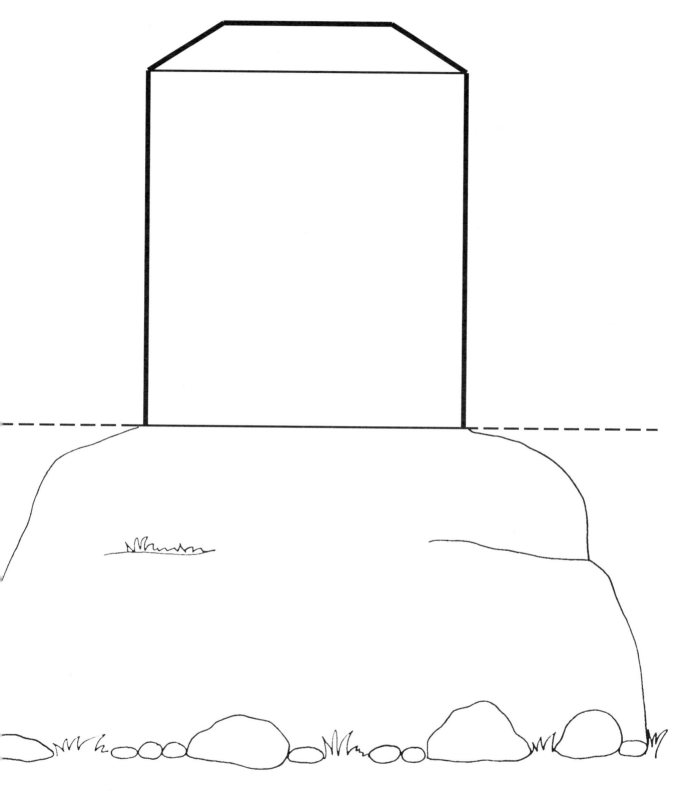

esus said,

nyone who hears these words of mine and obeys
em is like a wise man who built his house on a rock.'

Matthew 7:24

Lesson 10

Jesus Stills the Storm

Lesson aim: to teach that Jesus has control over nature because he is God.

Preparation

1. Read Luke 8:22-25.

2. Answer the following questions:
   * what happens to waves when the wind drops? If you do not know, half fill a washing up bowl with water and rock it from side to side to produce waves. Stop rocking the bowl and see how quickly the water becomes calm.
   * in the light of the above could this occurrence have been a coincidence?
   * who was the miracle for - Jesus' followers or the crowd?
   * what did the miracle demonstrate about Jesus?

3. Think about the power of Jesus' words. Note the similarity with God's word of creation (Genesis 1:3,6,9,11,14,20,24,26).

4. Ask God to help you teach this lesson simply and enjoyably.

5. Choose and prepare visual aids.

Start by asking the children if they can remember who they have been hearing about - Jesus. Remind them about the previous 2 lessons.

Today we are having another story about Jesus. Jesus was very tired. He had been telling the people about God and making lots of sick people better. It was evening and Jesus said to his friends, 'Let's go across to the other side of the lake.'

So they climbed into the boat. Because Jesus was very tired he lay down and fell fast asleep. The men were rowing over the calm water to the other side of the lake. Suddenly they noticed that the sky was getting dark, the wind was blowing and the waves were getting bigger. Very soon they were in the middle of a big storm. The waves were coming into the boat. How do you think they felt? They were all very frightened and Jesus was still fast asleep. They didn't know what to

do, but they knew that if they woke Jesus he would help them. So they woke Jesus and said to him, 'Don't you care that we are all going to drown?' Jesus stood up and said to the sea and the wind, 'Be quiet - be still!'

Immediately the wind stopped blowing and the waves calmed down. Jesus said to his friends, the disciples, 'Why were you so frightened, wasn't I with you?' Jesus' friends were astonished. 'Who is this person?' they said. 'Even the wind and the waves do as he tells them.'

Stress the lesson aim at this point.

Prayer

Dear Lord Jesus, thank you that you are always there to help us. Amen.

Visual aids

Either pictures from a Child's story Bible or make a boat out of cardboard box, using a broom handle for a mast and a tea towel for the sail. Use your arms to show where the oars would go. As you tell the story use the boat. Rock it when it gets rough. Tell the children to blow hard at the sail during the storm, and to blow softly when the storm calms down.

Activities

1. Each child requires page 31 photocopied on paper and 2 waves cut out of an A4 sheet of blue paper (see diagram).

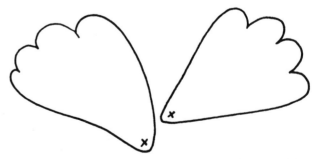

Prior to the lesson cut off the end strip from page 31. The children colour the picture. Attach the waves to the front of the picture with a split pin paper fastener at X. The waves move up to show the boat during the storm and down to show what happened when Jesus commanded the waves to be still.

2. Make a flag. Photocopy page 32 for each child. The children colour the picture, then glue the left side of the picture around a garden stick or length of dowel. Small pieces of blue paper can be glued onto the sea as a collage.

'Who is this man? He gives orders to the winds and the waves, and they obey him!'

Luke 8:25

"Who is this man? He gives orders to the winds and the waves, and they obey him!" Luke 8:25

Jesus Brings Jairus' Daughter Back to Life

Lesson aim: to teach that Jesus has control over death because he is God.

Preparation

1. Read Luke 8:40-42,49-56.

2. Answer the following questions:
   - who was Jairus?
   - what was his problem?
   - what caused Jesus to delay? (v.42-48)
   - was the girl really dead? (v.49,52-53)
   - what does this miracle demonstrate about Jesus?

3. Pray for the children you teach, asking God to open their eyes to who Jesus is.

4. Choose appropriate visual aids.

Start by finding out what the children can remember about the previous 3 lessons. Remind them that Jesus can forgive sin and control the wind and sea because he is God.

One day Jesus was in a great crowd of people. A man called Jairus came and knelt down before Jesus. Jairus was one of the chief men in the synagogue (or church). He had a little girl who was 12 years old. She was very sick. Jairus asked Jesus to go to his house and make her well again.

Jesus had started to go with Jairus when he was stopped by a very ill lady. While Jesus was making the ill lady well, a man arrived from Jairus' house. He told Jairus that his daughter had died. When Jesus heard this he told Jairus not to worry, only to believe that Jesus could heal her and his little girl would get better.

When Jesus arrived at Jairus' house he found all the people crying because they were so sad that the little girl was dead. Jesus said, 'Do not cry; she is not dead but only sleeping.' All the people laughed at Jesus, because they knew that the little girl was really dead.

Jesus went into the little girl's bedroom with his 3 friends, Peter, James, and John, and the girl's father and mother. He took the little girl's hand and told her to get up. Immediately she became alive again and got out of bed. Her parents were amazed.

Stress the lesson aim at this point.

Prayer
Dear Lord Jesus, thank you that you are God. Amen.

Visual aids
Pictures from a Child's Story Bible.

Activities

1. Photocopy page 34 for each child on card. Prior to the lesson cut along the thick black line round the figures. The children colour the figures. Fold the figures into a circle with the figures looking out and glue the base together so that the figures stand up.

2. Make a paper bag puppet for each child. Photocopy page 35 for each child. Prior to the lesson fold the sheet of paper in half and sellotape along the top and side to make a bag, open at the bottom. The children colour the faces.

Retell the story with the children pretending to be Jairus' daughter, using the puppet. While the little girl is ill and then dead the children place the hand with the puppet flat on a table or their lap with the *dead face* uppermost. When Jesus says, *'Little girl, get up'*; they hold up the puppet with the *alive face* showing.

The same thing can be done without the puppets and with the children lying on the floor pretending to be dead. When the little girl comes alive the children jump up and dance around. Why could Jesus do this? Because he is God.

Jesus said, "I am the resurrection and the life." John 11:25

fold line

Lesson 12

Jesus Feeds 5,000

Lesson aim: to teach that Jesus could perform miracles because he is God.

Preparation

1. Read Luke 9:10-17.

2. Answer the following questions:
   - where had the apostles been? (v.1-6)
   - what were the 2 parts of Jesus' ministry? (v.11)
   - what do verses 12-13 tell us about the disciples' faith? Is this surprising in the light of verses 1-6?
   - how many people were present? (v.14)
   - what does this miracle teach about who Jesus is?

3. Think about the disciples' lack of trust in Jesus' ability to provide for everyone's needs. Are you trusting God to supply your current needs?

4. Ask God to open the children's eyes to who Jesus is.

5. Choose and prepare visual aids.

Start by reminding the children of all the things they have been learning about Jesus.

One day Jesus was with his friends, the disciples. A great crowd of people came to find Jesus. *(To give the children some idea about the number of people present, take a building they all know, e.g. your church, and ask them to imagine it packed full of people standing up. It would be even more people than that - twice as many, three times as many, etc. depending on the size of the building.)* Jesus told the people all about God and he made the sick people well again.

It was getting late and Jesus' disciples came to Jesus. They told him that the people were very hungry and asked Jesus to send the people away to get something to eat. Jesus said to his disciples, *'You feed them.'* The disciples had no food to give to

so many people and no money to go and buy it. They did not know what to do.

There was a little boy in the crowd. He had a basket containing 5 bread rolls and 2 small fish. *(Place a basket containing 5 bread rolls and 2 card fish on a table.)* The disciples took the basket to Jesus. *'This is all the food we have,'* they said. *(Point out to the children the large size of the crowd and the small amount of food.)*

Jesus told the disciples to ask all the people to sit down. Then he took the 5 bread rolls and 2 small fish and gave thanks to God. He broke them into pieces and told the disciples to give them to all the people. *(Break a bread roll and hand a piece to each child.)* And everyone had enough to eat! In fact when they collected all the scraps there were enough to fill 12 baskets.

Stress the aim of the lesson at this point.

Prayer
Dear Lord Jesus, thank you for our food. Amen.

Visual aids
A basket containing 5 bread rolls and 2 small fish. Make the fish from light card covered with kitchen foil (see fish on page 37). Use proper bread rolls if possible.

You might like to have 12 pictures of baskets to pin up on a board. Ask the children how many baskets of food the disciples had at the start. Then ask them how many baskets of food were present at the end. Count the baskets aloud with the children.

Activities
1. Give each child a paper cup, some playdough (see the visual aids section on page 84), 2 fish cut out of card (see page 37) and 2 pieces of kitchen foil to cover the fish. The children make 5 bread rolls from the playdough and cover the fish with the kitchen foil. If wished, instead of using kitchen foil the fish can be covered with glue and glitter. To do this the children need to work on sheets of newspaper to catch the spare glitter. Place the bread rolls and fish in the paper cup. Give each child a sticky label with *'Jesus fed 5,000 people'* written on it to stick round the outside of the cup.

2. Give each child a paper plate with *'Jesus fed 5,000 people. Luke 9:10-17'* written round the rim. Before the lesson cut out 5 loaves and 2 fish from card for the children to glue onto the plate (see templates on this page). The children colour the loaves and fish. The fish can be covered with kitchen foil or glitter if wished (see activity 1).

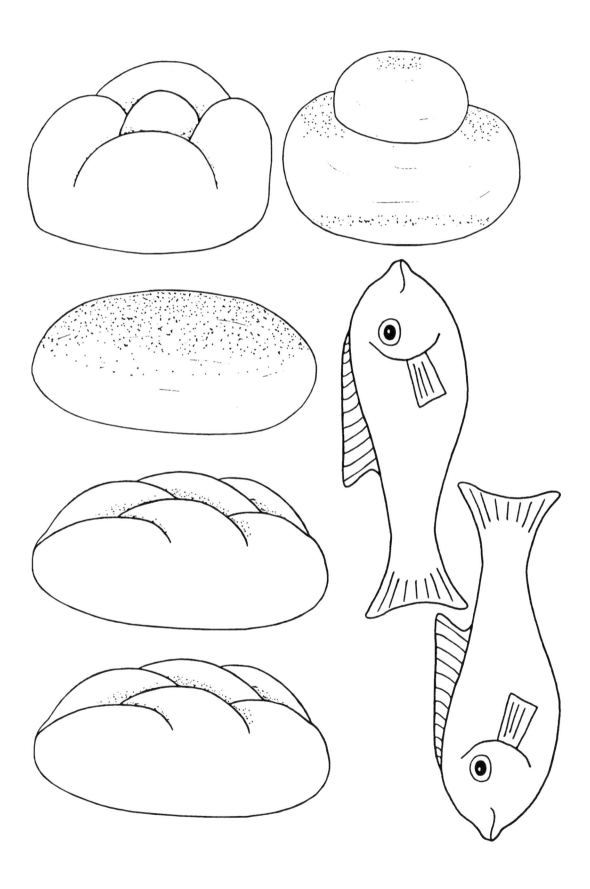

Lesson 13

The Parable of the Good Samaritan

> ## Lesson aim: to teach the children to be kind to everyone.

Preparation

1. Read Luke 10:25-37.

2. Answer the following questions:
   - who was asking Jesus a question? (v.25)
   - why was he asking the question? (v.25)
   - can anyone fulfil the criteria of verse 27 and justify himself? (see v.29)
   - do you know why it was so shocking that the Samaritan was the one who helped? Jews hated Samaritans and had nothing to do with them. The Law binding both Jew and Samaritan stated that their neighbour was their kinsman and countryman. Jesus' hearers would have understood that the man who was robbed was a Jew.

3. Think about the cost in time, money, effort and personal inconvenience to the Samaritan. Am I willing to spend these things in Jesus' service?

4. Ask God to help you teach the children clearly. It is important to stress the need to be kind without inferring that by so doing they will earn their way to heaven.

Remind the children of what they have been learning about Jesus. As well as making people well again, can anyone remember what else Jesus did? He told people about God and how they could be his friends. Often Jesus told the people stories. One day he told a story about how we should behave to other people.

Once there was a man travelling along a hot, dusty road. Suddenly, from behind some rocks, jumped a band of robbers. They were very bad men. They tore off the traveller's clothes and hit him with big sticks. The poor man fell to the ground. He hurt so much that he couldn't get up. It got hotter and hotter and as the man lay on the ground with a sore head he hoped that someone would come and help him.

Some time later a priest passed by. He was a very important person, but when he saw the man do you know what he did? He crossed to the other side of the road and left him lying in the hot sun.

A little later on another important man came along the road. He also crossed to the other side of the road and left the man lying on the ground.

Then later on a Samaritan came by. He came from another country. The man lying on the road was a Jew and Jews did not like Samaritans. When the Samaritan saw the man lying on the ground he got off his donkey. He bandaged the poor man's cuts and put him on his donkey. Then he took him to a house where people would look after the poor man.

Which one of the 3 men was kind to the man who had been robbed? Stress the lesson aim at this point.

Prayer

Dear Lord Jesus, please help me to be kind to other people. Amen.

Visual aids

Either pictures from a Child's Story Bible or models. If using models make peg people or yoghurt pot people (see the visual aids section on page 83). Also you need a toy donkey. If wished, use duplo figures or similar.

Activities

1. Make a stand-up figure of the good Samaritan. Photocopy page 39 on card for every 2 children. Fold the page in half along the dotted line and cut out the figure. The children colour the figure. Fold the tabs back along the dotted lines and glue together to form a base. The figure will stand up.

2. Make a booklet. Each child requires an A4 sheet of coloured paper and pages 40 and 41 photocopied back to back. Prior to the lesson fold the coloured sheet and photocopied sheet in half with the coloured sheet on the outside. Staple at the centre to form a booklet. On the front cover write: *The Parable of the Good Samaritan Luke 10:25-37*. On the back cover write: *Jesus said, 'Go and do the same.' Luke 10:37*. The children colour the booklets.

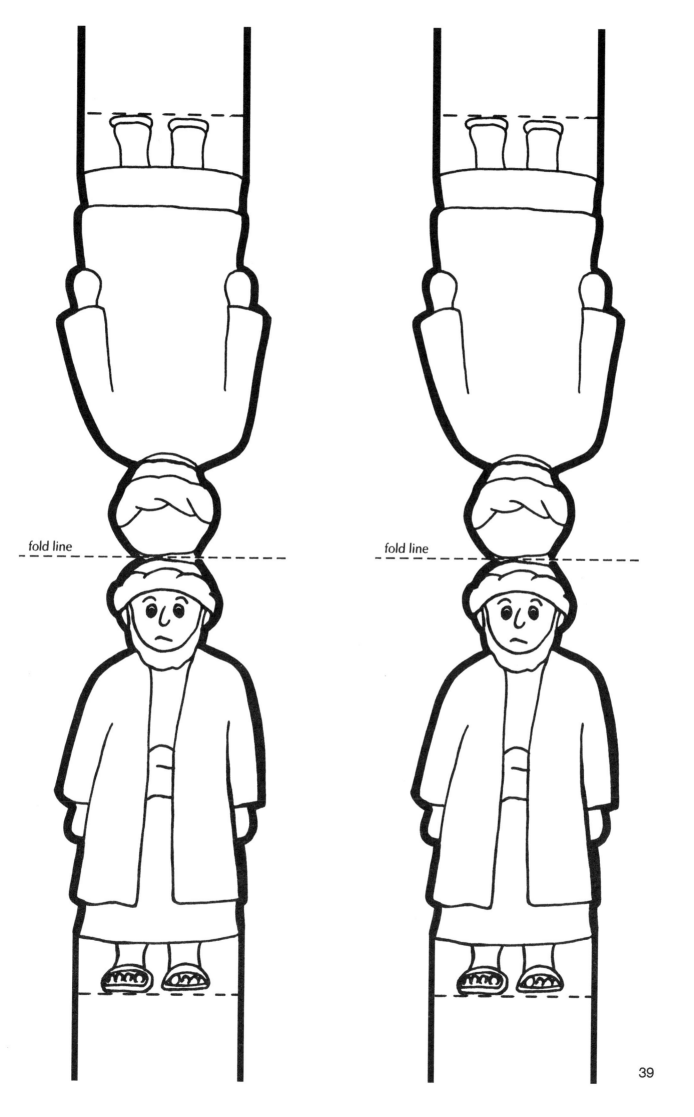

fold line

fold line

Jesus told the following story.

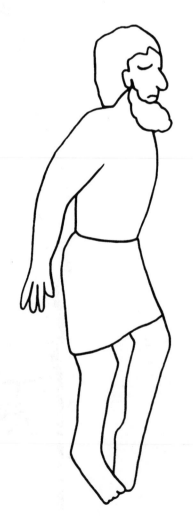

A traveller was set upon by robbers. They took his belongings, beat him and left him lying by the road.

Finally a Samaritan came along. He bandaged the man's cuts, put him on is donkey and took him to a house where people would look after him.

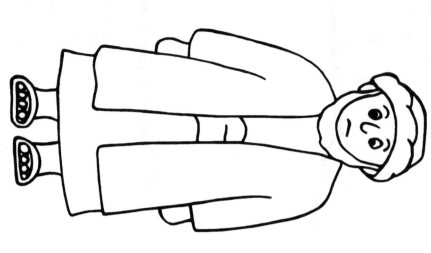

Which one of the 3 men was kind to the man who had been robbed?

A little later a man who worked in the temple passed by.

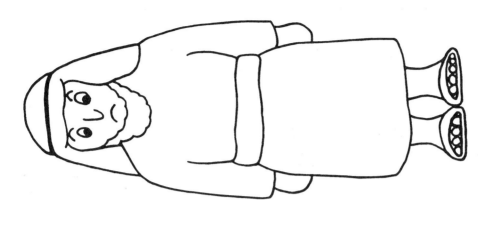

He went over to the man and looked at him, then went on his way.

Some time later a priest passed by.

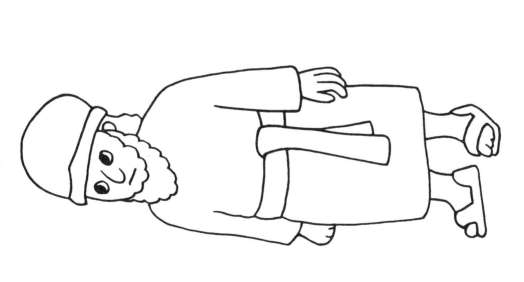

He saw the man lying in the road and crossed over to walk on the other side.

41

Lesson 14

The Parable of the Lost Sheep

Lesson aim: to learn that God loves each one of us and does not want anyone to be separated from him.

Preparation

1. Read Luke 15:3-7.

2. Answer the following questions:
- who was Jesus talking to (v.1-2)?
- who searched for whom - the shepherd for the sheep or the sheep for the shepherd?
- why did the shepherd and his neighbours have a party?
- what does this parable teach about the importance of the sinner to God?
- is there anyone who does not need to repent?

3. Pray for each child you teach, asking God to help them understand how much Jesus loves them.

4. Choose appropriate visual aids.

Remind the children that they have been learning about Jesus. Jesus often told people stories to help them learn about God. This is one of the stories Jesus told.

There was a man who had lots of sheep, one hundred in all.

They were all different, just like we are. Some were big, some were small; some were fat, some were thin; some were light and some were dark. The shepherd knew each of the sheep by name.

One day the shepherd woke up and realised that one of his sheep was missing. He left the 99 sheep which were safe, and went to look for the lost sheep. He looked and looked, and in the end he found the lost sheep, which was all alone. Then the shepherd picked up the sheep and carried it home.

When he got back the shepherd was so happy at finding his lost sheep that he decided to have a party. He invited all his friends to be happy with him, because he had found the sheep that was lost.

Jesus said that God is like that shepherd. He loves each one of us and does not want anyone to be away from him. And God is really happy when anyone comes to him and says they are sorry for all the naughty things that they have done.

Prayer
Dear Lord Jesus, thank you for loving each one of us, just like that shepherd loved his lost sheep. Amen.

Visual aids
Either pictures from a Child's Story Bible or figures to pin onto a board.
You need a picture of a large flock of sheep (large numbers such as 99, 100 mean very little to children of this age), cut outs of a single sheep, some rocks and several bushes. Hide 1 sheep behind a bush before the lesson starts.
If the class area is large enough you could hide a toy sheep and get the children to find it.

Activities
1. A model sheep.
   Materials: - paper roll centres cut to size, match sticks, playdough, egg box, cotton wool, glue, sellotape, marker pen.
   Instructions:
- Cut the cardboard tubes approximately 7 cm long, 1 for each child.
- With sellotape attach a section of an egg box to one end of the tube for the face. Draw on 2 eyes with the marker pen.
- Make four small holes in the underside of the body for the match stick legs and attach the match sticks.
   NB The match sticks must be lit before being used.
   If necessary, stick the legs into blobs of playdough to help the sheep stand up. The children glue cotton wool over the body.

2. A sheep pendant.
   Photocopy page 43 onto card for each child. Cut out the pendant and draw 4 legs on the back. Punch a hole at X and thread a loop of wool

42

through the hole big enough to go over the child's head. The children glue cotton wool balls onto the front of the sheep and colour the area around the legs on both sides green.

The Parable of the Lost Son

Lesson aim: to teach the children that God forgives those who are truly sorry.

Preparation

1. Read Luke 15:11-32.

2. Answer the following questions:
   - did the younger son show any love for his father? (v.12-13)
   - what made the younger son come to his senses?
   - what picture are we given of the father?
   - what did the younger son do to obtain forgiveness?
   - what are we told about the younger son's relationship with his father following his return?

3. Pray for each child in your class, asking God to help you teach them the importance of saying sorry to Him for wrongdoing.

4. Choose appropriate visual aids.

Remind the children that they have been learning about some of the stories Jesus told to help people learn about God. See if they can remember anything about the good Samaritan or lost sheep. One day Jesus told the following story.

There was a man who had two sons. This man was very rich and lived on a farm. Both sons helped on the farm. The younger son did not like this. He wanted to go to the big city and enjoy himself. So he asked his father for his share of the money. His father gave it to him and the son went off to the big city.

In the city he made a lot of new friends. The son spent his time going to parties and buying new clothes. Soon all his money was spent. After all his money had gone he had nothing to eat, so he got a job as a pig-keeper. He didn't get enough money to buy food for himself. He was so hungry that he would have eaten the pig's food. No one gave him anything to eat. He was very, very sad.

One day he thought, *'My father has lots of servants and they all have enough to eat. I will go to him and tell him how sorry I am for all the wrong things I have done, and ask him to make me one of his servants.'* So he got up and went home.

As he got near to his father's house, his father saw him coming. His father was so pleased to see him that he ran to meet him and hugged and kissed him. The son told his father how sorry he was and that he was no longer worthy to be his son. But his father called to the servants to bring new clothes for his son. The father gave a big party, because he was so pleased his son had come back.

Stress the lesson aim at this point.

Prayer
Dear Lord Jesus, help us to say sorry to you whenever we are naughty. Amen.

Visual aids
Pictures from a Child's Story Bible.

Activities

1. Discuss with the children the sort of things they do that are wrong. Point out that we all do naughty things - even their parents and teachers. Try and get the children to be specific about things they have done that week. When we are naughty we make God very sad. We have to say sorry to the person we have wronged (give examples) and to God. If I say sorry to God he forgives me. That means that he will make things right again and forget that I did that naughty thing. But I must be really sorry and try not to do that naughty thing again. Finish with a time of prayer, encouraging the children to pray simple one sentence prayers.

2. Photocopy page 45 for each child. Concertina fold along the dotted lines so that the father moves towards the son. The children colour the picture.

against God and against you.
Luke 15:21

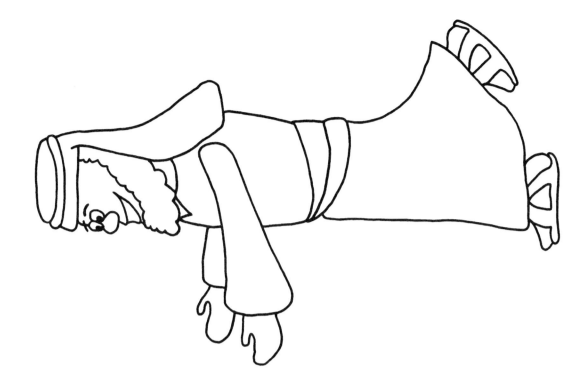

Father, I have sinned

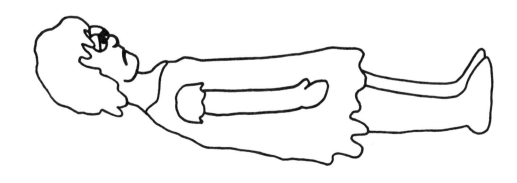

Lesson 16

Jesus Heals Ten Lepers

Lesson aim: to teach the children to thank God for all the good things he gives us.

Preparation

1. Read Luke 17:11-19.

2. Answer the following questions:

- where was Jesus? (v.11)
- what probable nationalities were the ten men? (vv.11,16)
- what did the men ask Jesus to do?
- why did Jesus tell them to show themselves to the priests? (Leviticus 14:1-2)
- what were the lepers demonstrating by going to the priests?

3. All ten were healed, but only one came back to say thank you. Think about how you can teach the children the importance of saying thank you to God for all the good things he gives us.

4. Pray for the children in your group, asking God to help you teach them to be thankful.

5. Choose appropriate visual aids.

Remind the children that they have been learning about Jesus and the wonderful things he did. Ask them if they can remember anything Jesus did. They will probably need a lot of prompting.

One day Jesus was on a journey when he met 10 men who were very sick. They had very sore skin. Nobody wanted to go near them in case they got sick too. The men were very sad.

When they saw Jesus they called out and asked him to help them. Jesus told them to go and show themselves to the priests. This is what people with sore skin had to do when they were made better.

The men did what Jesus told them. They went off to the priests. On the way they saw that they had been made well. Straight away one of them turned back, praising God out loud.

When he got back to Jesus he bowed down before him and thanked him. Jesus said to him, *'Were not 10 men healed? Where are the other 9?'*

Stress the lesson aim at this point.

Prayer

Dear Lord Jesus, thank you for all the good things you give us. Amen.

Visual aids

10 finger puppets (see page 84) or a concertina strip of 10 men (see diagram). Colour the faces with blotches of pink and brown. If you are using a concertina strip break off the end one to come back and say thank you.

Activities

1. Point out that only one of the 10 said thank you. Discuss with the children what sort of things we should say thank you to God for, e.g. parents, homes, friends, etc. Finish with a time of prayer, encouraging the children to say simple one sentence prayers.

2. Teach the children the finger rhyme:

   10 sick men came to Jesus one day.
   (hold up 10 fingers and thumbs)
   Jesus made them better as he sent them all away.
   (both hands behind back)
   Nine of them ran off so happy to be new,
   (hold up all fingers and 1 thumb)
   Only one remembered whom to say thank you to.
   (stick up the other thumb)

3. Make a set of chain-men for each child. Concertina fold a strip of paper to make 10 men. Draw on faces apart from the mouths. Let the children help draw happy mouths on the men. Each child requires a sticky label with 'Thank you' written on it. Ask the children how many men said thank you. Each child chooses which man said thank you and sticks the label onto his body. The men can be coloured.

Jesus Heals a Blind Man

> **Lesson aim: to teach that Jesus can make a blind man see because he is God.**

Preparation

1. Read Luke 18:35-43.

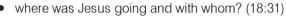

2. Answer the following questions:
- where was Jesus going and with whom? (18:31)
- why was Jesus going? (18:31-33)
- what did the blind man know about Jesus? (v.37-38)
- what did Jews understand by the term, "Son of David"? (Jer 23:5-6, Ezek 34:23-24, Lk 20:41-44)
- what did the blind man want Jesus to do? (v.41)
- what did Jesus say healed the man? (v.42)
- what was the result? (v.43)

3. Think about where Jesus was going and why. Yet he had time for a man of no account - a blind beggar. Think about how you can teach the children about the love and compassion of Jesus and how his actions demonstrated he is God.

4. Pray for the children you teach, that they will recognise Jesus is God and, like the blind man, respond to him in faith.

5. Choose appropriate visual aids.

Remind the children they have been learning about the wonderful things Jesus did. Talk about last week's story - the healing of the 10 lepers. Our story today is about another sad man who needed Jesus' help.

One day Jesus was on a journey. He was surrounded by a great crowd of people, walking along with him. Sitting by the road side was a blind man. (Check that the children know what it means to be blind.) The blind man heard the noise of all the people passing by. He called out to ask what was happening. The people told the blind man that Jesus was passing by. The blind man called out to Jesus to help him. Some of the people told the blind man to be quiet, but he cried out all the more, *'Jesus, help me!'*

Jesus stopped and asked the people to bring the blind man to him. Then Jesus asked him what he wanted. The blind man asked Jesus to make him see. Jesus said, *'Receive your sight, your faith has made you well.'* Immediately the man could see. He followed Jesus, praising God. And all the people, who saw the man healed, praised God also.

Stress the lesson aim at this point.

Prayer
Dear Lord Jesus, thank you for making that blind man see. Thank you for showing us that you are God. Amen

Visual aids
Pictures from a Child's Story Bible.

Activities
1. Photocopy page 48 for each child. Cut off the top strip with the arrow. Cut out the eye sockets and cut along the dotted lines either side of the face to make slots. Slot the strip into place, feeding from the left, so that the eye sockets are empty and the eyes are to the left of the sockets. Pull the tab to the right to make the man 'see'. The children colour the pictures.

2. Play *I Spy* – 'Who can see something green?' 'Who can see a flower?' etc.

3. Retell the story with the children playing the part of the blind man. They all close their eyes until Jesus made the blind man see. Then they open their eyes, jump up and praise God.

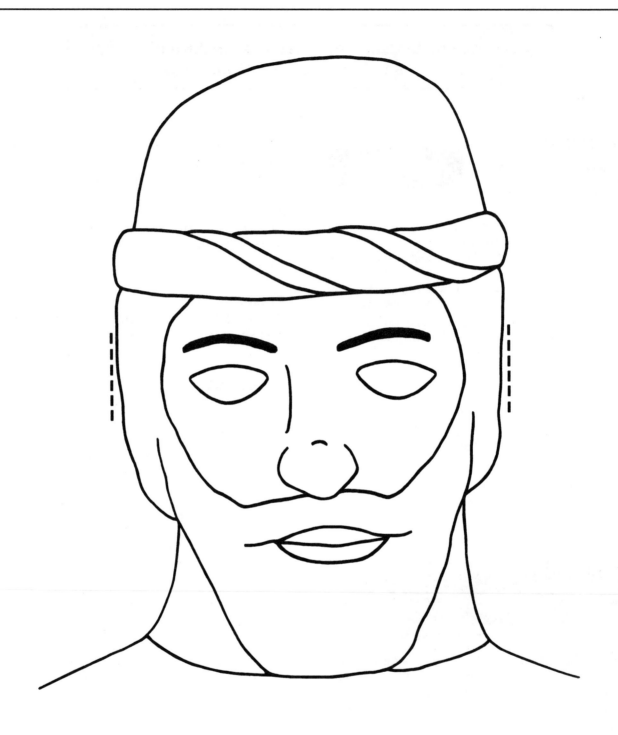

Jesus said, 'Receive your sight.'
Luke 18:42 (NIV)

Jesus Rides into Jerusalem

> **Lesson aim:** to teach that Jesus is King and worthy of our worship.

Preparation

1. Read Luke 19:28-40.

2. Answer the following questions:
   - why was Jesus going to Jerusalem? (18:31-33)
   - Jesus gave his disciples specific instructions (v.30-31). How do v.32-33 confirm who Jesus is?
   - what would the crowd have understood from Jesus riding on a donkey? (Zechariah 9:9, cf. Matt 21:5)
   - why did the Pharisees want Jesus to rebuke his disciples?

3. Think about the crowd's reaction to Jesus. One week later they would be shouting, *'Crucify him!'* (Luke 23:13-13).

4. Pray for the children you teach, that they may understand that Jesus is a great king, who knew what would happen to him.

5. Choose appropriate visual aids.

Remind the children that they have been learning about Jesus. Talk about Jesus being able to do what he did because he is God. Point out that most people did not know this.

Jesus was on his way to Jerusalem with his friends. Just before they got there Jesus sent 2 of his friends to a nearby village to fetch the donkey they would find. They went to the village and found the donkey, just like Jesus said.

They brought the donkey to Jesus. His friends spread coats over the donkey for Jesus to sit on.

Off they all went to Jerusalem. Jesus rode on the donkey and his friends walked behind. There was a big crowd of people there. As Jesus rode along, they placed coats on the road in front of the donkey.

As Jesus entered Jerusalem the people began to wave branches and praise God for all the mighty things they had seen Jesus do.

Stress the lesson aim at this point.

Prayer

Dear Lord Jesus, thank you that you are a great king. Thank you that you know everything. Amen

Visual aids

Pictures from a Child's Story Bible.

Activities

1. Photocopy page 50 for each child on card. Fold the page in half along the dotted line and cut out the donkey along the thick black line, being careful **not** to cut across the fold line at the top of the ears. The child colours the donkey and glues the base together so that the donkey stands up.

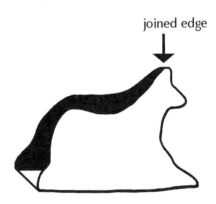

joined edge

Provide small leaves and bits of material for each child to glue under the feet of the donkey.

2. Help the children to act out the story.

Jesus Dies and Comes Back to Life

Lesson aim: to teach that Jesus died on the cross to take the punishment for my sin.

Preparation

1. Read Luke 23:32 - 24:9.

2. Answer the following questions:
   - had Jesus done anything wrong? (v.22,40-41)
   - if Jesus was God could he have come down from the cross and saved himself? (v.35,37,39)
   - why did he choose to stay there? (Romans 5:8-10)

3. Think about what it cost Jesus to save you and how much God loves you. How can you demonstrate your love for him?

4. Pray for each child you teach, asking God to help you love them and teach them.

5. Choose and prepare visual aids.

Remind the children that they have been learning lots of wonderful things about Jesus. See if they can remember any of them. Who is Jesus? Jesus is God. Remind them about Jesus entering Jerusalem on a donkey.

Jesus taught many people the truth about God. The priests became very angry because the people listened to Jesus and did not listen to them.

The priests sent soldiers to arrest Jesus. Jesus was put to death. Jesus, who never did anything wrong, died to take God's punishment for all the wrong things **we** do.

After Jesus died he was put into a cave and a big stone was rolled across the entrance. A soldier guarded the cave to make sure no one went in.

Two days later, when a few of Jesus' friends went to the cave, they found that Jesus' body had gone.

Two angels appeared and told them that Jesus had come back to life, just as he had promised. This showed that Jesus was the Son of God.

Prayer

Dear Lord Jesus, thank you for dying on the cross so that we can be your friends. Thank you that you are alive for ever. Amen.

Visual aids

Pictures from a Child's Story Bible. You can also make a garden scene using a plastic margarine container for the cave, white cloth, stone, twigs, etc. and yoghurt pot or peg people (see page 83).

Activities

1. Stand up cave card

   Photocopy page 52 on card for each child. Fold along the dotted line and cut out the cave, being careful not to cut along the dotted line. Open out the cave and cut out the doorway. Close the cave and write, *He is risen! Mark 16:6* on the back of the cave so that it is visible through the doorway. Cut out the stone, angel and strips for attaching the stone from a single thickness of card. Attach the 2 short strips of card with staples to the inside of the card front so that the strip of card attached to the stone can be threaded through them (see diagram on page 52). Staple the long strip of card to the back of the far side of the stone (see diagram on page 52).

   The children colour the cave, stone and angel. Glue the angel inside the cave to the left of the verse. Thread the strip attached to the stone through the strips on the back of the cave front. Show the children how to pull the stone back to open the doorway. **NB** The stone sits in **front** of the opening.

2. Make an Easter garden with the children. Each child needs a yoghurt pot half full of damp sand or earth, some twigs or leaves, 2-3 flowers and a cardboard cross with *He is risen!* written on it. If sand or earth are not available you can use play dough instead (see recipe on page 84).

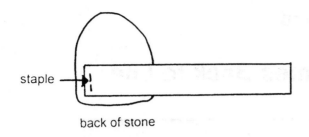

staple →

back of stone

inside of cave front

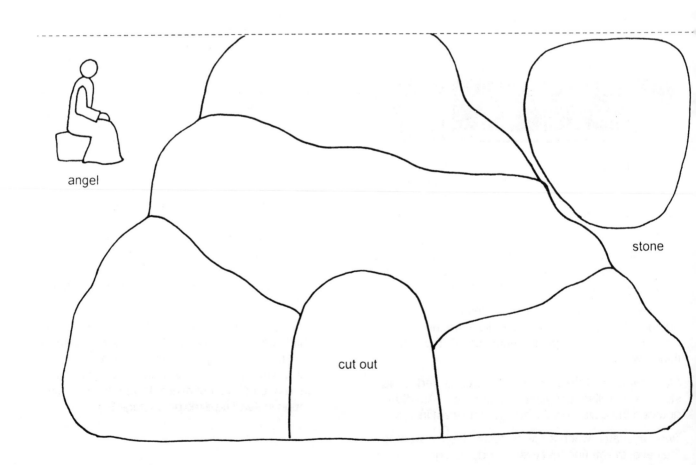

angel

stone

cut out

strip to attach to stone

The Road to Emmaus

> **Lesson aim: to show that Jesus is alive and was seen by witnesses after his resurrection.**

Preparation

1. Read Luke 24:13-35.

2. Answer the following questions:
   - on which day were the men going to Emmaus? (v.1)
   - had the men got their facts right? (v.18-24)
   - what was their problem? (v.25-27)
   - at what point did the men recognise Jesus? (v.30-31)
   - from this passage how do we know Jesus was alive and not a ghost or a product of their imagination?

3. Pray for the children you teach, asking God to open their eyes to who Jesus is.

4. Choose and prepare visual aids.

Remind the children of the 2 previous lessons - Jesus entering Jerusalem and his death and resurrection.

That same evening 2 of Jesus' friends were walking home from Jerusalem. They talked about Jesus and all that had happened. They were very sad that Jesus had died. They knew that Jesus' body wasn't in the cave, but they did not know what had happened to it.

A man approached them and walked with them. They did not know who he was. While they walked along he told them why Jesus had to die.

Soon they came to their home. The men asked the stranger to come in for a meal. All 3 went into the house and sat down at the table. *(Sit all the children round a table.)*

The stranger said thank you to God for the food, then handed it around. Then the men recognised that the 'stranger' was Jesus.

Suddenly Jesus disappeared. The 2 men ran back to Jerusalem to tell Jesus' friends what had happened. *'Jesus is alive!'* they said, *'We have seen him.'*

Prayer

Dear Lord Jesus, thank you that you are alive for evermore. Amen.

Visual aids

Either pictures from a Child's Story Bible or act out the story with the children as it occurs. Put a light cloth over the head of the child playing Jesus so that he is not recognisable. You need bread for them to break at the table. Remove the cloth from the head of 'Jesus' as the bread is passed around.

Activities

1. Photocopy page 54 for each child to colour.

2. Photocopy this page and page 55 for each child. Prior to the lesson cut out the 2 men from this page. Using a needle and cotton attach the 2 men to the picture. Starting at the **back**, insert the needle through the X at the left side of the picture, then from back to front through the X at the rear of the figures, through the X at the front of the figures, and through the X at the right of the picture. Tie the 2 ends of cotton at the back of the picture. The 2 men move along the cotton from Jerusalem to Emmaus.

The Lord is risen. Luke 24:34

On the Sunday after Jesus died 2 of his friends were walking to Emmaus. They were very sad.

A stranger went with them. He explained why Jesus had to die and rise from the dead. The 2 men did not realise that the stranger was Jesus. (Luke 24:13-35)

55

Ascension and Pentecost

Lesson aim: to teach that Jesus has sent his Holy Spirit to be with his people.

Preparation

1. Read Luke 24:36-53, Acts 1:1-11; 2:1-11.

2. Answer the following questions:
   - how did the disciples prove Jesus was real and not a ghost? (Luke 24:38-43)
   - can we understand the Scriptures without God's help? (Luke 24:45)
   - what message must be preached to all nations? (Luke 24:47)
   - for what were the disciples to wait? (Luke 24:49, Acts 1:4-5)
   - what would the Holy Spirit empower the disciples to do? (Acts 1:8)
   - in Acts 2:1-4 we read about the first giving of the Holy Spirit to the New Testament believers. Why were physical signs necessary?
   - what did the Holy Spirit enable the disciples to do? (Acts 2:4-11, cf. Acts 1:8)

3. Think about the commission Jesus gave to his disciples. Thank him for the privilege of teaching his word to children.

4. Choose appropriate visual aids.

Remind the children of the previous 2 lessons about Jesus' death and resurrection and his appearing to the 2 men on the road to Emmaus.

After Jesus died and came back to life again, his friends the disciples saw him many times. One day he took them to the top of a hill outside Jerusalem. He told them to stay in the city until God sent the Holy Spirit to be with them. The Holy Spirit would help them tell everyone they met about Jesus. After Jesus had finished speaking he disappeared into a cloud and the disciples could not see him. Jesus had gone back to heaven to be with God. Then the disciples went back to the city and waited for the Holy Spirit to come just as Jesus had promised.

Some time later there was a special holiday called Pentecost, when people came to Jerusalem from other countries to worship God. The disciples were sitting together in their room praying. Suddenly there was a noise like a great wind and a flame appeared and seemed to touch each person. God's Holy Spirit had come.

The Holy Spirit made them able to talk in other languages. This allowed the disciples to tell the people from other countries all about Jesus.

Prayer

Dear Lord Jesus, thank you for giving us your Holy Spirit to help us do the things that please you. Amen.

Visual aids

Either pictures from a Child's Story Bible or enlarge and colour the pictures used for the story box on page 57.

Activities

1. Make a story box.
   Photocopy page 27 on card for each child, having changed the title to read, 'Ascension and Pentecost Luke 24:36-53, Acts 1:1-11; 2:1-11'. Photocopy page 57 on paper for each child. Make up the boxes following the instructions on page 27. Cut out the 4 pictures from page 57 and place in an envelope for each child.
   The children colour the pictures and glue them round the box in the order of the story.
   Use the story box to revise the story.

2. Photocopy page 58 for each child. Prior to the lesson cut out red flames from gummed paper for the children to stick over the heads of the disciples (see diagram). The picture can be coloured.

Ascension and Pentecost

Jesus told his friends that he would send his Holy Spirit to help them tell people about Jesus.

Then a cloud took him out of their sight. Jesus had gone back to heaven.

The Holy Spirit came to be with Jesus' friends, just as Jesus had promised.

The Holy Spirit helped them tell other people about Jesus.

Jesus promised to send his friends his Holy Spirit.

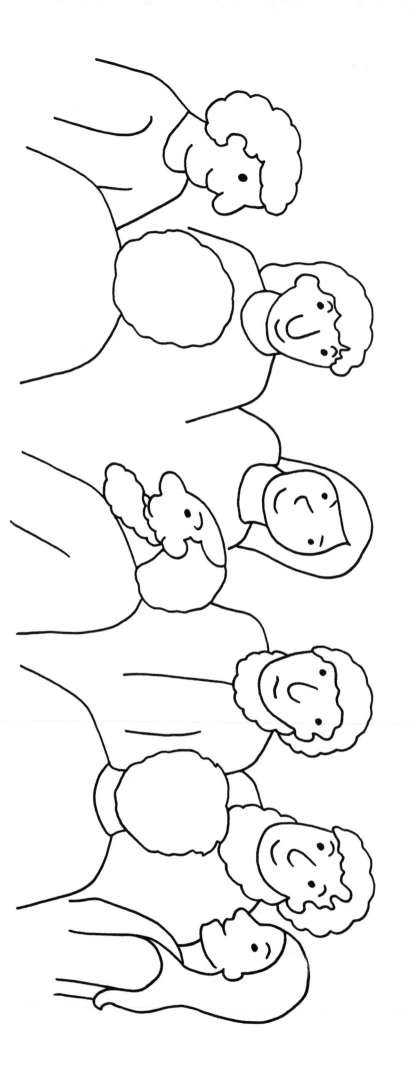

The Holy Spirit came, just as Jesus had promised.   (Acts 1:1-11; 2:1-11)

Peter and the Lame Man

> **Lesson aim: to teach that Jesus' followers were able to perform miracles because they had the Holy Spirit.**

Preparation

1. Read Acts 3:1-10.

2. Answer the following questions:
   - how long had the man been lame? (v.2)
   - how long did it take to heal the man? (v.7)
   - who healed the man? (v.6,12,16)
   - what was the result of the miracle? (v.8-10; 4:4)

3. Think about the miracle and its end result. Would the people have listened to Peter's message if they had not seen the miracle? What caused the people to believe - seeing the miracle or hearing the message?

4. Ask God to help you teach the story simply and clearly.

5. Choose appropriate visual aids.

Remind the children of the previous lesson - the coming of the Holy Spirit. Ask them what special job Jesus gave to his disciples - to tell other people about him. Two of Jesus' friends were called Peter and John. One day they went to the temple to pray.

A lame man was sitting at the gate, asking people for money. *(Explain what it means to be lame.)* He asked Peter and John for money. Peter told him that they had no money to give him, but that they could give him something much better. Peter said to the man, *'In the name of Jesus Christ, get up and walk.'* Then Peter took the man's hand and lifted him up. Straight away the man was able to walk. The man went with them into the temple, to praise God for healing him. All the people who saw what happened were amazed. Then Peter told the people about Jesus.

Prayer

Dear Lord Jesus, thank you that you used Peter to make that lame man better. Amen.

Visual aids

Pictures from a Child's Story Bible.

Activities

1. Act out the story, with the children taking the various parts.

2. Photocopy page 60 on card for every 2 children. Cut out the man and his 2 legs. Using split pin paper fasteners attach the legs behind the body where marked, making sure that the legs move freely. Attach a length of fine elastic to the head of the man so that he will dance.
   The children colour the man. Fold his legs up for sitting and down for walking.
   Remind the children that it was Jesus who healed the man.

3. Photocopy page 61 for each child. Before the lesson cut out the lame man. The children colour the picture and glue the lame man at the foot of the steps.

Peter and the Lame Man

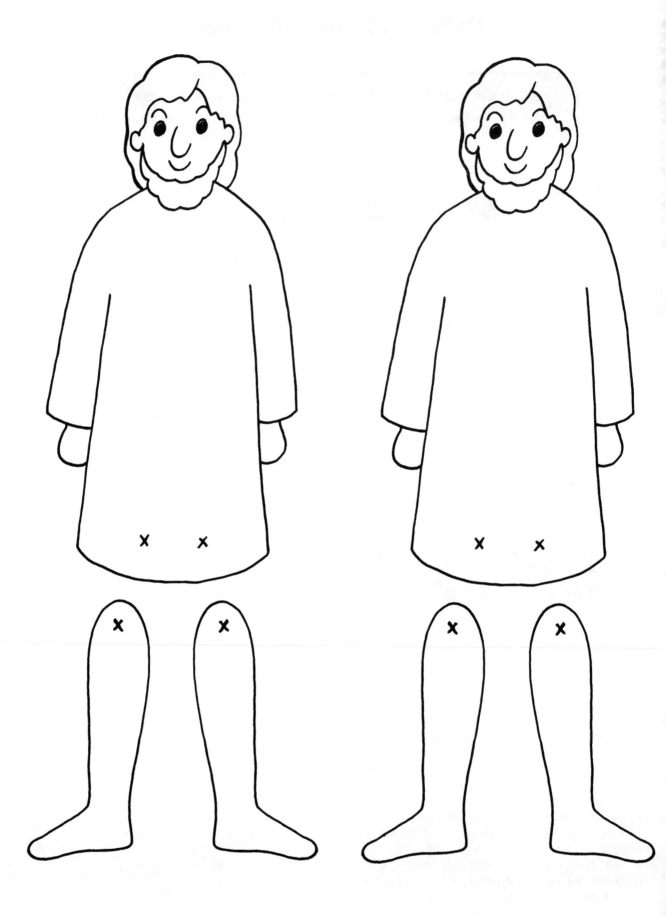

Peter and John met a lame man at the temple steps.

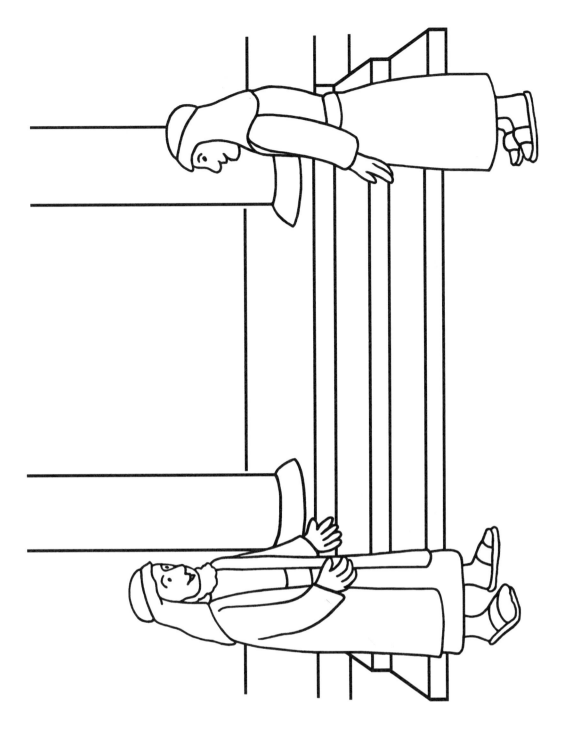

Peter said, "In the name of Jesus Christ of Nazareth I order you to get up and walk!"   Acts 3:6

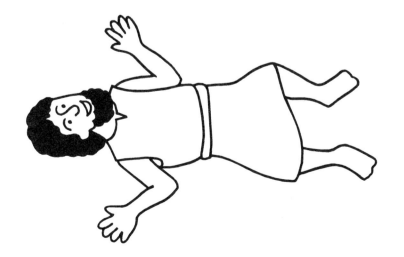

Peter and Dorcas

Lesson aim: to show that God has control over death.

Preparation

1. Read Acts 9:36-42.

2. Answer the following questions:
   - what did Dorcas spend her time doing? (v.36)
   - was Dorcas really dead? (v.37)
   - what was the result of the miracle? (v.42)

3. Pray for the children you teach that they may put their trust in the Lord Jesus.

4. Choose appropriate visual aids.

Start by asking the children if they can remember the names of Jesus' 2 friends from the previous lesson. Today we are having another story about Peter. Who can remember what happened to Peter last time? Remind the children about the healing of the lame man at the temple.

There was a lady called Dorcas, who lived in a busy seaside town called Joppa. In the hot afternoons she sat sewing in the shade by her house. She enjoyed making clothes for people. Dorcas had many friends. When someone needed help they came to her. Dorcas told people about Jesus.

One day Dorcas felt very ill. She had to stay in bed. After a few days she died. Her friends all came to her house. They were very sad.

Peter, one of Jesus' friends, was in a village not very far away. Dorcas' friends sent a message to Peter, asking him to come quickly to the house. Peter came to the house and was shown to a room upstairs where Dorcas lay.

Peter knew how sad Dorcas' friends felt. He asked them to leave him alone. Peter knelt down and prayed and asked Jesus to help him. Then he told Dorcas to get up. Straight away Dorcas opened her

eyes and got up. Jesus had brought her back to life. Peter called her friends back. How happy they were!

All over Joppa people talked about the way Jesus showed his love for Dorcas by bringing her back to life.

Ask the children if they can remember Jesus bringing anyone back to life when he was on earth. Remind them about Jairus' daughter.

Prayer

Dear Lord Jesus, thank you that you look after us and help us. Amen.

Visual aids

Pictures from a Child's Story Bible.

Activities

1. Photocopy page 63 for each child. Prior to the lesson cut off the strip containing Dorcas. Cut out Dorcas and cut a slit along the thick black line on the bed. Cut off the section of strip above Dorcas' head. Insert the tail end of Dorcas through the slit so that she is lying in the bed with her head on the pillow. Take the cut-off section of strip and place it over the body of Dorcas on the back of the picture. Sellotape it to the back of the picture to make a pocket. Dorcas can lie down and be pulled out to sit up. The children colour the picture.

2. Make a pendant. Photocopy page 64 on card for each child. Cut out the 2 circles and glue them together so that there is a picture on both sides. Make a hole at X using a hole punch. Thread a piece of wool through the hole and join at the ends. The wool loop must be big enough to go over the child's head.

Dorcas was dead. Peter asked Jesus to make her better.

Dorcas came alive again. Many people believed in Jesus. (Acts 9:36-43)

pocket

Peter prayed to Jesus.

Jesus made Dorcas better.

Lesson 24

Peter Escapes from Prison

Lesson aim: to show that God has control over all our circumstances.

Preparation

1. Read Acts 12:1-11.

2. Answer the following questions:
   - why was Peter in prison? (v.1-3)
   - how was Peter guarded? (v.4)
   - how did the Christians react to Peter's imprisonment? (v.5)
   - how was Peter released?   List all the miraculous details. (v.6-10)

3. Think about the way God looked after Peter. How has God looked after you during the last week?

4. Ask God to help the children understand that he looks after them.

5. Choose appropriate visual aids.

Remind the children of the previous 2 lessons about Peter. Peter went about telling the people about Jesus. The priests did not like this, so the king put Peter in prison.

The Christians prayed to God for Peter. One night, as Peter slept chained between 2 soldiers, an angel appeared. *'Wake up, Peter,'* he said. Peter woke up, but the soldiers stayed asleep.

Peter's chains fell off. The angel told Peter to put on his sandals and cloak. Peter did so and followed the angel out of the prison.

The angel took Peter past the soldiers and when they got to the gate to the outside of the prison it opened all by itself. The angel took Peter out of the prison then the angel disappeared.

Peter thanked God for sending the angel to set him free.

Prayer

Dear Lord Jesus, thank you for looking after Peter. Thank you for looking after us each day. Amen.

Visual aids

Pictures from a Child's Story Bible.

Activities

1. Photocopy page 66 for each child. Cut around 2 sides of the door and cut out the window between the bars. Fold the page in half with the picture on the inside. Put a split pin into the outside of the door as a handle. The children colour the picture and draw in chains on the floor at Peter's feet.

2. Mark off an area of the room to be the prison. Designate 1 or more children to be soldiers and the rest to be Peters. When the soldiers tag a Peter he/she has to go to prison. The prisoner can be released if 1 of the free children acts as an angel and tags the imprisoned child without being caught by the soldier(s).

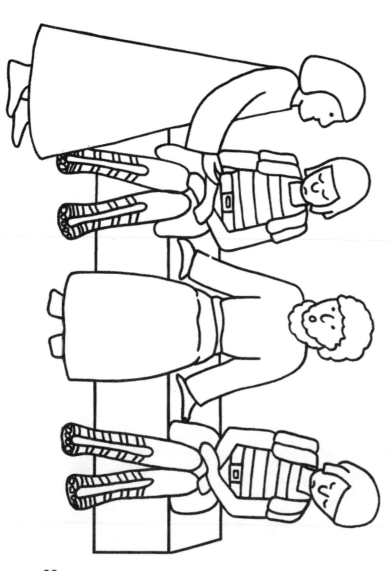

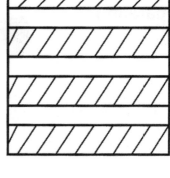

Peter said, 'The Lord sent his angel to rescue me.'   Acts 12:11

Lesson 25

Paul Becomes a Christian

> **Lesson aim: to learn that conversion involves a change of heart and behaviour.**

Preparation

1. Read Acts 9:1-20.

2. Answer the following questions:
   - what does the Bible tell us about Saul? (Acts 7:57 - 8:3; 22:3, Philippians 3:5-6)
   - when does his name become Paul? (Acts 13:6-13)
   - why was Saul going to Damascus? (9:1-2)
   - who saw the light and heard the voice? (v.3-7)
   - why did God choose Saul? (v.15-16)
   - how did Saul change following his conversion?

3. Think about the change God wrought in Saul's life. Look back over your own life. Have you changed to become more like Jesus?

4. Pray for the children you teach that they might put their trust in the Lord Jesus.

5. Choose appropriate visual aids.

Throughout this lesson we will refer to Saul as Paul, because this is less confusing for small children.

After Jesus died the priests tried to stop people becoming followers of Jesus. There was a young man named Paul. He followed the Jewish Law and was careful to do everything it said.

Paul was sent to a city called Damascus to arrest all Jesus' followers and take them back to Jerusalem. Paul hated these Christians.

Suddenly, on the way to Damascus, a bright light shone from heaven. Paul fell to the ground and heard Jesus speak to him. Jesus told Paul to go to Damascus where he would be told what to do. When Paul got up he was blind.

After Paul arrived in Damascus he prayed to God. God sent a follower of Jesus to Paul to put his hands on him. Paul could see again.

Then Paul was baptised and met with the other Christians.

After Paul became a follower of Jesus he changed. Instead of hating Christians he loved them. He didn't want to punish Christians any more, instead he wanted to tell people about Jesus so they could become Christians too.

Discuss with the children what difference being Jesus' friends should make in their lives, e.g. wanting to do the things that please God, wanting to speak to God, wanting to learn about him, etc.

Prayer
Dear Lord Jesus, please help us to do what pleases you. Amen.

Visual aids
Pictures from a Child's Story Bible.

Activities
1. Make a paper hand puppet for each child plus one for the teacher. Photocopy page 68 for each child. Cut off the puppet and fold in half along the dotted line. Sellotape along the top and side to make a bag, open at the bottom. In front of the children, draw a sad mouth on one side of the puppet and talk about Paul before he became a Christian. Then turn the puppet over and draw a happy mouth, talking about the change in Paul after he became a Christian.
   Help the children to draw a sad mouth on one side and a happy mouth on the other side of their puppets. The children colour the puppets and glue on strands of wool for hair.
   Ask the children to put their puppets on their hands. Ask them to show Paul before he became a Christian. Talk about him being very angry and hating Christians. Then get the children to turn the puppet around to show Paul after he became a Christian. Talk about the change in Paul - happy and loving his fellow Christians.

2. Make a cone figure of Paul. Photocopy page 9 on card for each child. Prior to the lesson cut out

the appropriate pieces and place in an envelope for each child.

The children colour the pieces. Help them fold the body into a cone shape and glue it together.

Place the head on the body by placing the long tab through the hole at the top of the cone. Staple or glue the base of the tab to the inside of the body front. Glue on the head-dress.

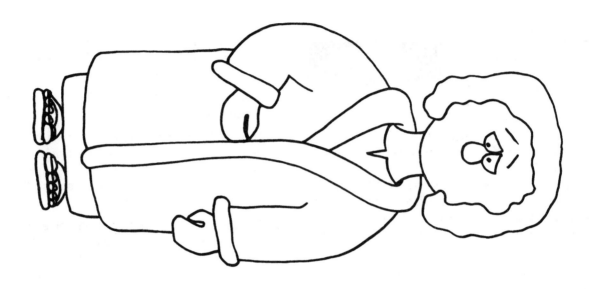

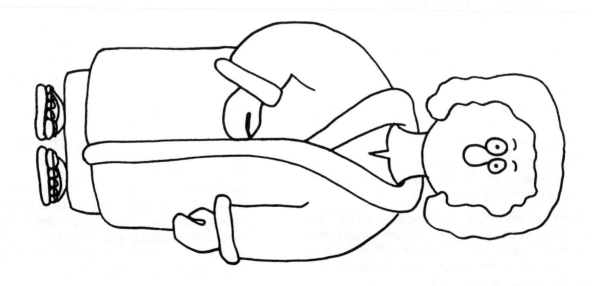

The Philippian Jailer Becomes a Christian

Lesson aim: to teach that conversion results in a changed life.

Preparation

1. Read Acts 16:16-34

2. Answer the following questions:
   - was the slave girl telling the truth? (v.17)
   - why were Paul and Silas imprisoned? (v.19-23)
   - what did the jailer need to do to be saved? (v.29-32)
   - how did the jailer change following his conversion?

3. Pray for the children you teach, asking God to help them live lives that please him.

4. Choose appropriate visual aids.

Start by reminding the children of the previous lesson - Paul's conversion. Paul and another Christian called Silas were going to lots of different places to tell people about Jesus.

In one city the people became very angry and asked the rulers to punish them. Paul and Silas were beaten and put in prison. The jailer made sure they could not escape.

During the night Paul and Silas were praying and singing to God. The other prisoners were listening. Suddenly there was a great earthquake and everything shook.

All the prison doors flew open and every prisoner's chains fell off. The jailer woke up and thought all the prisoners had escaped. He picked up his sword to kill himself. Immediately Paul called out to stop him. Paul told him all the prisoners were still there.

The jailer was surprised to find the prisoners had not run away. He asked Paul how he could be saved. Paul told him to believe in Jesus.

The jailer took Paul and Silas to his own house and gave them a wash and clean clothes. Paul told the jailer and his family all about Jesus and how they could be God's friends because Jesus had died on the cross and rose from the dead. The jailer and his family believed what Paul told them and became Christians.

At the end of the lesson remind the children of last week's lesson - Paul, who hated Christians and tried to punish them, was changed into someone who told people about Jesus so that they could become Christians. When the jailer became a Christian he changed, just like Paul. Before he was a Christian the jailer threw Paul and Silas into prison and tied them up with chains. When he became a Christian he washed their wounds and gave them something to eat.

Prayer

Dear Lord Jesus, please help us to believe in you, just like the jailer did. Amen.

Visual aids

Pictures from a Child's Story Bible.

Activities

1. Make a booklet. Photocopy pages 70 and 71 back to back for each child. Cut the page in half and fold the 2 halves together to form a booklet. Staple together at the fold.
   The children colour their booklets. Go through the booklet with the children.

2. Make a musical shaker. Each child requires a paper cup or cardboard tube, rice/macaroni/dried peas, and a piece of colourful wrapping paper. Seal one end of the container. The children place the dried materials into the container, which is sealed with cling film. Glue a piece of wrapping paper round the container. Remind the children that the jailer and his family were filled with joy when they believed in Jesus. Sing a simple praise song, using the shakers.

He and his family
were filled with joy,
because they now
believed in God.

Acts 16:34

into

sad people

butterflies

caterpillars

into

glad people

into

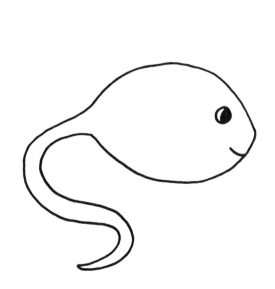

tadpoles

frogs

Paul is Shipwrecked

Lesson aim: to teach that God looks after the people who love him.

Preparation

1. Read Acts 27:1-44.

2. Answer the following questions:
   - why didn't the army officer listen to Paul's advice? (v.9-12)
   - why was Paul confident that the sailors and passengers would survive? (v.21-26)

3. Think about God's power and the way he controlled circumstances to get Paul to Rome. Do you trust God enough to let him order your life?

4. Thank God for giving you the privilege of teaching children. Ask him to help you teach his word accurately and clearly.

5. Choose appropriate visual aids.

Remind the children about the previous 2 lessons - Paul's conversion and the conversion of the Philippian jailer. Many years later Paul was imprisoned by the rulers because he was always telling people about Jesus. They sent Paul to Rome so that the king could decide whether he should be punished. It was a long way and he had to go by ship.

A great storm arose which lasted for many days. The thunder rolled and the lightning flashed, and everyone on the ship was very afraid. They thought that they would drown.

One night God spoke to Paul in a dream and told him that everyone on the ship would be saved. Paul believed God and told the people on the ship what God had said.

A few nights later the sailors realised that the water was getting shallower. They were afraid that the boat would strike some rocks so they lowered the anchors. Then, after having something to eat, they threw all the remaining food and goods into the sea to lighten the boat.

The following morning the people on the ship saw that they were close to land, so they tried to sail into the beach. When they got as close as they could, those who could swim to shore did so, and the others held on tightly to bits of wood from the boat. Everyone got safely to land, just as God had promised.

Prayer

Dear God, thank you for looking after Paul. Thank you for looking after us every day. Amen.

Visual aids

Pictures from a Child's Story Bible.

Activities

1. Make a calm/stormy sea scene. Photocopy pages 73 and 74 for each child. Prior to the lesson cut out the boat and sea along the thick black line.
   The children colour the boat and background page.
   Fasten the boat to the background through the centre of both with a split pin paper fastener. The background can be moved so that the boat will have first a calm background, then a stormy one, ending with a calm one. Talk to the children about God looking after Paul.

2. Discuss with the children how God looks after us, e.g. giving us food and water, homes to live in, parents to look after us, etc. Talk about the importance of saying thank you to God for giving us these things. End with a time of prayer, encouraging the children to say simple one sentence prayers.

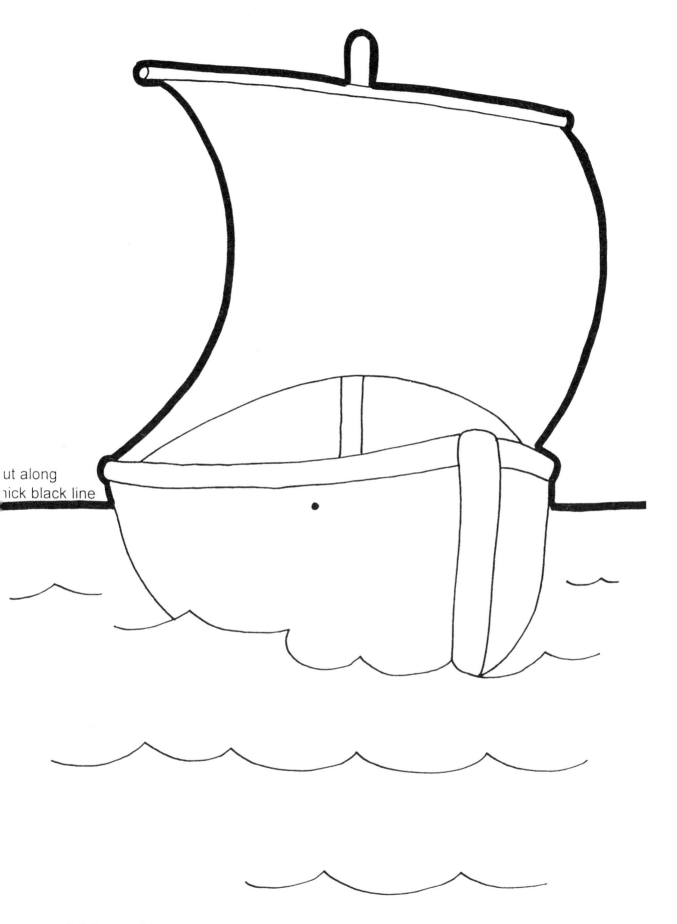

ut along
nick black line

We all got safely to shore. Acts 27:44

Zacchaeus Becomes a Follower of Jesus

> **Lesson aim: to teach that Jesus came to save sinners.**

Preparation

1. Read Luke 19:1-10.

2. Answer the following questions:
   - what do we learn about Zacchaeus?
   - why did the crowd grumble?
   - why did Jesus call people lost?

3. Think about the way Jesus cared for people who, for various reasons, were despised. Thank him for coming to save the lost.

4. Ask God to help you teach the children about his love for them.

5. Choose appropriate visual aids.

Remind the children of all the wonderful things they have been learning about Jesus (lessons 8,-12, 16 & 17). One day Jesus and his friends were passing through a town called Jericho.

A man called Zacchaeus lived in Jericho. He was very rich, but had made his money by cheating other people. The people of Jericho did not like him. Zacchaeus had heard about Jesus and wanted to see him. Zacchaeus was only a small man. There were so many people crowding around Jesus, that Zacchaeus could not see him. So Zacchaeus ran on ahead and climbed up a tree so that he could see Jesus when he walked by.

When Jesus came to the tree he looked up at Zacchaeus and asked him to come down, because Jesus was going to stay at his house. Zacchaeus hurried down the tree and took Jesus to his house. Zacchaeus was so happy. But the people who were there grumbled. They could not understand why Jesus would go to a bad man's house to stay. (Stress lesson aim.)

Zacchaeus told Jesus that he would give half of his money to the poor and he would also give money back to the people he had cheated.

Prayer

Dear Lord Jesus, thank you that you want us to be your friends. Amen.

Visual aids

Pictures from a Child's Story Bible.

Activities

1. Photocopy page 76 on paper and page 77 on card for each child. Cut along the dotted lines at the top and bottom of page 76 and around the left hand side of the tree to make a flap. Cut out the figure of Zacchaeus and the 2 tab extensions. Attach the extensions to both ends of Zacchaeus. The children colour Zacchaeus and the tree. Slot the tab ends through the top and bottom of the page so that Zacchaeus can be moved up into the tree and down again, passing under the cut out flap on the tree.

2. Make a headband for each child. Photocopy page 78 on card for each child. Cut out the 2 pieces and staple or sellotape together at one end.   The children colour and decorate their headbands with gummed paper shapes and stars. Fit the headband onto the child's head and staple or sellotape the 2 ends together.

The Son of Man came to seek and to save the lost.   Luke 19:10

attach to top tab
on figure

attach to bottom
tab on figure

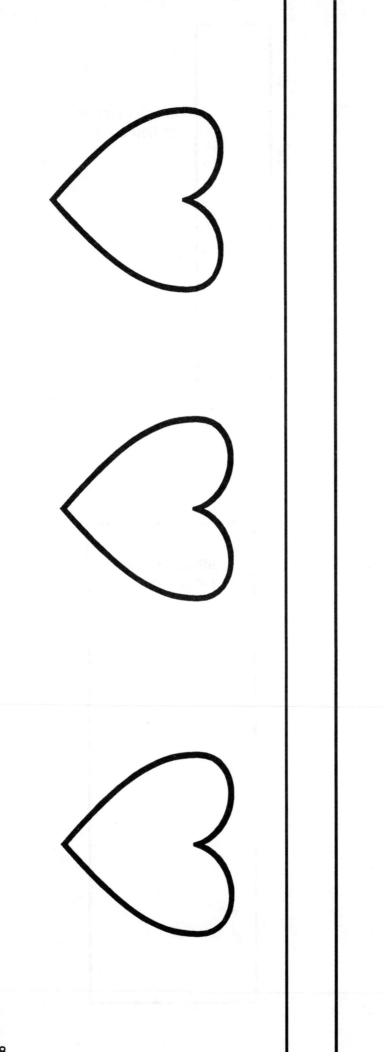

Jesus is my Saviour.

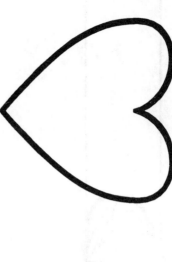

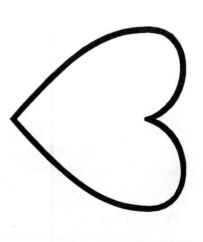

The Transfiguration

Lesson aim: to teach that Jesus is the Son of God and we must listen to what he says.

Preparation

1. Read Luke 9:28-36

2. Answer the following questions:
   - what had happened a week earlier? (v.18-27)
   - what were Moses and Elijah discussing with Jesus? (v.31)
   - whose voice came from the cloud? (v.35)
   - what does this passage teach about Jesus? (v.35)

3. Think about how we listen to Jesus through his word, the Bible. Do you read it regularly?

4. Pray for the children you teach that they will realise the importance of learning from God's word, the Bible.

5. Choose appropriate visual aids.

Prayer

Dear Lord Jesus, please help us to learn about you from your Word, the Bible. Amen.

Visual aids

You may not be able to find this story in a Child's Story Bible. Photocopy pages 80 and 81 to use as a visual aid. Cut out the figures from pages 80 and 81, colour and glue onto card. If you want to use a picture of Jesus, cut out another man. Cut a piece of kitchen foil the same size as Jesus' robe to put on Jesus when he is transfigured. Cut out the cloud and colour. Pin the figures onto a board as you tell the story.

Activities

1. Photocopy pages 80 and 81 for each child. Cut out the cloud from page 81. The children colour the picture. Glue the tab on the top of the cloud behind the top of page 80 so that the cloud can be pulled down to cover Moses and Elijah.

2. Photocopy page 82 for each child on card. Cut out the mask and the eye holes. Attach a length of shearing elastic to both sides of the mask. The children decorate their masks. Point out to the children that when Jesus was on the mountain his appearance was changed. Putting a mask on changes their appearance.

Remind the children of all the wonderful things they have been learning about Jesus (lessons 8-12). One day Jesus took 3 of his friends, Peter, James and John, up on the mountain to pray. Jesus started to pray, but his 3 friends went to sleep.

While Jesus was praying his face and clothes shone. Two men, Moses and Elijah, came from God to talk with Jesus about his dying on the cross.

Suddenly Jesus' friends woke up and saw him all shining and talking to Moses and Elijah. As they watched a cloud came over them and they were very frightened. God spoke from the cloud and said, *'This is my Son, listen to him.'*

Then Moses and Elijah disappeared and Jesus was standing all alone. (Stress the lesson aim at this point.)

Jesus took Peter, James and John up a hill
to pray. Suddenly 2 men were there talking
with Jesus. They were Moses and Elijah.

Mask

Visual aids

Yoghurt Pot People

Requirements

Yoghurt pots or plastic drinking cups, egg cartons, scraps of material, wool, rubber bands, cotton wool, sellotape, glue, pens.

Instructions

Cut the head from an egg carton and sellotape onto a yoghurt pot or plastic cup. Draw on a face. Dress with a piece of material secured round the middle with wool or a rubber band. Tuck the bottom edge of the material inside the bottom of the pot. Attach the head-dress in similar fashion to the robe. Glue on cotton wool as a beard if required.

Peg People

Requirements

Wooden clothes pegs, scraps of material, pink or white paper, card, bluetak, pipe cleaners, cotton wool, needle and thread, glue, pens.

Instructions

1. Wind a piece of paper around the top of the clothes peg and draw on a face.

2. Wrap a pipe cleaner around the peg just below the face and make a loop at each end for the hands.

3. Cut out a length of material twice the length of the peg and approximately 5 cm wide. Make a slit at the centre big enough to go over the top of the peg. Place the material over the top of the peg (see diagram).

4. Wrap the material round the peg and use ½ a pipe cleaner as a belt.

5. Make card feet (see diagram) and attach to the base of the peg with bluetak.

6. Take a square of material approximately 6 x 6 cm to make the head-dress. For a man, attach the head-dress using ½ a pipe cleaner as a head band. For a woman, turn in the top edge of the material then wrap it round the face, securing it with a stitch.

card feet

83

Finger Puppets

Instructions

1. Using the templates (see below), cut out a body and arms. Draw on a face, head-dress, clothes and hands and colour appropriately. The arms and hands should be coloured on both sides.

2. Roll the body into a tube and glue the back together along the dotted area.

3. Glue the arms onto the back of the body (see diagram).

Playdough

Ingredients   2 cups plain flour
2 cups water
1 cup salt
2 dessert spoons cooking oil
2 oz cream of tartar
food colouring

Mix all the ingredients together in a large saucepan and cook over a low heat, stirring constantly, until the mixture forms a stiff dough. This takes 5 - 10 minutes. Turn the dough out onto a board or work top and knead until the dough is easily malleable. Wrap the dough in cling film and leave to cool. Periodically take the dough out of cling film and knead to remove the crust that forms as it cools. Once the dough is cold give it a final knead and replace in fresh cling film. The dough can be stored wrapped in cling film in an airtight container, e.g. ice cream container, for up to 6 months.